Tangled in
TINSEL

ISBN: 9798767443840 (print)

BLURB

This Christmas took an unexpected turn, and left me all tied up...

I thought landing my dream job in the city was a Christmas wish come true, until a freak snowstorm prevented me from going home for the holiday. Trying to kick my bah-humbug mood, I ventured out in search of festivities.

What I found was Mason Reed.

The ten years since we last saw each other has been good to him, turning the awkward teen I once knew into a man who oozes sex and charm. The idea of being snowed in with Mason has visions of his sugar plums dancing through my head...

But Mason is keeping a secret that is sure to land him on the naughty list, and it involves the locked chest at the foot of his bed. That's one gift I don't want to wait until Christmas morning to open.

Stoke the fire, and hang the mistletoe, I have plans for Mason sure to make Santa blush. Yet when that box of goodies is finally cracked open, will it be more than I bargained for? Or leave me tangled up in desire?

Tangled In Tinsel is a Christmas quickie that will fill your stocking with lots of steamy goodness! This friends-to-lovers, second chance, holiday romance is sure to get you on Santa's naughty list!

ONE

QUINN

No! No, no, no! This seriously can't be happening to me! I'm so frustrated and mad right now I can barely stand it! I finally got my dream job that I worked so hard for, and even moved to the city early to get a head start on my new position. But then this happens, and I'm so upset.

Tilting my chin to the ceiling and blowing out a loud, agitated sigh, I close my eyes and try my best to hold the tears back. But unfortunately, there's nothing I can do about my current situation, and wallowing in a pity party certainly isn't going to help me. I can pout if I want to, but I'm still stuck here.

And *here* is not the worst place to be, but it's not where I want to be right now. I'm standing in a gorgeous apartment that's been beautifully decorated by my fantastic new employer, and all I can think is: *I wish I were somewhere else.* And now I feel like an ungrateful brat, because people would kill for a fabulous apartment like this right in the middle of downtown.

Pulling back my newly hung curtains, I look out the window at the blanket of white covering the city. It'd be the perfect winter wonderland if it didn't ruin my Christmas plans. But of course, mother nature just had to be that fickle bitch she's known for being.

My cell phone rings on the coffee table, the noise annoying me in my angry state. I quickly snatch it up to find out who's calling. Flipping it over, I see that it's my mom, and my demeanor immediately softens. I'm so lucky to have such an amazing mom, who really is my best friend. I know she already knows what I'm about to say, but that doesn't make it any easier.

"Hi, Mama Bear," I answer with a resigned tone.

"How's my Baby Bear?" Her voice is tentative, telling me she's already seen the news.

"I'd be doing a hell of a lot better if I were on the road right now, headed back home. But I can tell by your tone you've already seen the weather report, so you know I'm not coming."

"Yes, your father saw it this morning. So, I guess that means you won't be home for Christmas, then?" There's a trace of hope in her voice, but she and I both know it would be impossible for me to make it home for the holiday with this much snow.

Damn you, Jack Frost! Okay, get it together, Quinn. Now, you're cursing imaginary winter sprites. I shake my head at my foolishness.

"I'm so mad right now, Mom. You know how hard I've worked to get here, and I was so excited to start this new job. I moved down here early, so I could get a jump on things.

"Of course, that was with the stipulation that I could go home for Christmas and start my position right after the holidays. But who knew that over a foot of snow would be dumped on the city overnight, and I'd be stuck here?" I start pacing across the floor, trying to walk off some of my frustration.

"I'm sorry, honey. I know you were hoping to get home for Christmas, and your father and I will miss you terribly. We'll wait to celebrate until you can come home."

"Don't be silly, Mom. There's no need to wait for me to come home. I'm an adult, and I can celebrate the holiday by myself." This is the first and only time I've ever been away from home for Christmas, but I don't want my mom to hear how disappointed I am to not be with her and Dad. I know I may be an only child, but I'm 27 years old. I don't have to spend the holiday with my parents, even though it breaks my heart not to.

"I know you're an adult, but you'll always be my Baby Bear. And this is our favorite holiday—I can't make sugar cookies and peanut butter fudge without you. Who's gonna drink peppermint hot chocolate with me while watching the lights twinkle on the tree on Christmas Eve? Or drive around with me to look at all the Christmas lights? There's no way your father and I are going to celebrate without you. I wanna wait until you can be with us."

I anticipate doing our holiday traditions all year. It's the only time I can actually feel like a kid again, and I hate that I'm going to miss it. "You really don't have to do that, Mom, but I appreciate it anyway." I can hear the defeat in my own voice and try my best to sound a little more cheerful. "Are you at least going to cook our holiday dinner for you and Dad? I know he looks forward to all the food as much as I do every year."

"I'm sure I'll make something for your father and me, but I'll save our traditional holiday meal for when you come home. But what about you? What are you going to eat? Do you even have groceries yet?" It's just like my mom to always be in worry mode.

"No, not really. I only grabbed a few things because I didn't plan to be here for very long, since I was going to head home for Christmas. So basically, I just have the bare minimum. There's a bar and grille around the corner, so I'll pick up some takeout for tonight. And then I'll probably walk to the market down the street to buy a few things to get me through the rest of the week. Hopefully, by then, the snow will have cleared, and I can be home for New Year's."

"I just hate to think of my baby girl down there in that big city all by herself, spending the holiday all alone. It just breaks my heart!" I can hear my mother sniffle, and I know she's beginning to cry. Which, of course, makes me tear up as I'm already so tenderhearted right now. But I put on a brave face, so I don't upset my mother any more than she already is.

"I promise I'm gonna be just fine, Mom. I'm going to go ahead and get some dinner for tonight, and then I'll call you tomorrow for Christmas Eve. Give Daddy a big hug and a kiss for me, and I'll talk to you guys later. I love you, Mom."

"I love you too, Baby Bear. Take care of yourself and

know that I'm thinking about my precious girl. I'll talk to you tomorrow."

I hang up the phone, feeling homesick and sad. I can be as mad as I want to be, but that still won't change the fact that I'm not going home for Christmas. I mean, it wasn't like my new employer forced me to move down here the week of the holiday. And it certainly isn't their fault we suddenly got hit with shitty weather.

We're used to getting snow in upstate New York, but no one was prepared for this much of it, this fast. And now, I'm stuck here in a new city where I don't know anyone, spending the holiday all alone.

This Christmas sucks ass!

MASON

I'VE BEEN COMING TO CEDAR STREET AT LEAST ONCE OR twice a week for the last couple of years. It's a nice little neighborhood bar, and the food is actually pretty decent. Most of the time, I come here with some of the guys from work, but not tonight. No, it looks like I'll be spending tonight alone, doing my best to avoid Avery's advances while I try to eat my dinner in peace.

She's usually a little flirty with whatever male patrons come in, but that's not surprising considering she makes a living on tips. However, when it comes to me, she seems to always lay it on extra thick. I know she's trying to get more than a tip out of me, but I'm really just not interested. I have... particular tastes, and not just any woman can satisfy them. Even if she's a pretty girl like Avery.

I try to keep my head down while I eat my meal, pretending to be interested in something on my phone or whatever game is on the TV behind the bar. But that doesn't seem to stop her from touching my hand or trying to shove her tits in my face any chance she gets. I do my best to be polite, but I like coming here way too much to shit where I eat.

The front door opens, and a burst of cold air blows in, reaching all the way to the bar where I'm sitting. I look to see who has arrived, but the light reflecting off the mounds of white snow outside practically blinds me. I can tell whoever has walked in is female by the shapely figure approaching me. I can't see her face, but the way her curvy hips move in her skin-tight jeans has my mouth watering just to get a taste.

Her short, puffy black parka is pulled snugly around her, hiding the rest of her body from me. But I can already tell this girl has an hourglass figure, and I'm dying to get my hands on it after just one look. My reaction to this girl is very unusual for me, as there aren't many women who catch my eye so quickly. So, before I can start drooling over her luscious body, I turn my attention back to my meal.

She sits one barstool away from me and unzips her coat, pulling it off and laying it on the empty seat between us. From my peripheral, I see her spear her hands into her long, curly black hair as she rests her elbows on the bar and sighs in frustration. I watch Avery give her a once-over and smirk to myself when I see a glimmer of envy flash in her eyes. I haven't seen our newcomer's face yet, but I can tell from Avery's reaction she must be beautiful.

"What can I get you?" There's a hint of snark in Avery's question.

"Can I just have a bourbon for right now? Neat, please. Oh, and a menu." She has the most angelic voice I think I've ever heard, but there's also a familiarity to it. If I didn't know any better, I'd swear I've heard that voice before.

"Sure thing. I assume you'd like something to go?" I hold in my chuckle as I see right through Avery's ploy. It's obvious she wants this girl to leave and views her as crowding in on her territory. But I don't know how many ways I can say it nicely—I'm just not interested in Avery.

"Actually, I've decided to have my meal here. This seems like a nice place, so I think I'll stay awhile." The girl's voice is saccharine sweet, but there's no mistaking the "I'm not putting up with your bullshit" vibe she's giving off. And I must say, I find that quite the turn-on.

Avery pours her drink and sets it down in front of her along with a glass of water. I still can't see her face because her thick, glossy hair hides it from me. But I watch as she pushes the water aside and downs her bourbon in one shot. It's not often you see a woman walk into a bar and do that, so honestly, I'm a little impressed. I've only known one girl who drinks bourbon like that, and I haven't seen her in years, sometime after high school, maybe.

She sets her empty glass down on the mahogany bar and taps the rim, signaling for Avery to bring her another. She looks over her menu for a few moments before turning her head to look in my direction. Now that I can finally see her face, I'm absolutely stunned.

Her perfectly smooth, caramel-colored skin graces a gorgeous face with full, pouty lips coated in shiny clear gloss. She's not wearing a stitch of makeup, but it's the most beautiful gray-blue eyes with thick black lashes staring back at me that have me wholly enraptured—because I haven't seen them in almost ten years.

TWO

QUINN

As if my situation couldn't get any more frustrating, I'm now dealing with some mean-girl bartender as she shoots me dirty looks from the other end of the bar. When I walked in, it almost seemed as if I was interrupting something between her and the man sitting next to me. But if that's the case, he sure is doing an excellent job of ignoring her, as she continues to look at him longingly between shooting daggers in my direction.

I just want to get something decent to eat and a few drinks, in hopes it will help me forget that I can't see my parents for the holidays. I really don't need to put up with anyone else's bullshit right now, and I'm certainly not going to put up with hers. Or maybe I'm just being a bitch because I can't go home for Christmas, and I should cut her some slack. I'll decide later after a few bourbons.

I down my first drink in one shot, because that's how I always start off drinking, then I'll sip the rest of them as the evening goes on. The sweet oaky taste with undertones of vanilla and spice immediately fills my mouth as

9

the burn of the alcohol slides down my throat. The first drink is always the best one.

I let the bartender know I'd like another as I look over the reasonably extensive menu, considering this is a neighborhood bar. Usually, places like this only have a limited list of items. So, I'm surprised to see a menu that's several pages long. There're quite a few choices here, and some things are marked as local favorites. Maybe I should just ask someone for a recommendation, but it certainly won't be the girl who's serving me drinks tonight while shooting laser beams out of her eyeballs.

I glance up in the mirror behind the bar to get a better look at the man one seat away from me. As soon as I walked in, my eyes immediately went to him. Even though he's sitting down, I can tell he's tall—at least over six feet. And my God, this man has muscles for days. It's such a noticeable contradiction to his business attire, which includes a classic white button-down and dark gray slacks that mold perfectly to his body.

His dark hair is cut into a fade around the sides and the back, but it's a little longer on top. It's slightly tousled, as if he's been running his fingers through it—my fingers are itching to do the same. But it's his whiskey-colored eyes that steal my attention. I've seen those eyes before, and I'd know them anywhere.

"Mater?" I ask him with caution. I know I'm not mistaken, but just to be on the safe side, I call him by the nickname I'd given him so many years ago. When the corners of his mouth turn up into a smile, I know right away *it's him*.

"Quinn Parker." Dear Lord in heaven, this man has a

voice that could make a nun sin. He definitely didn't have a voice like that back in high school. The sound is deep but soothing and has an air of confidence without coming across as cocky. "Of all the bars, in all the cities, you just had to walk into mine?" His smile is playful, and I practically want to burst into giggles like a little schoolgirl.

"Mason Reed. My little Mater. What are you doing here?" I've known this man for years, and we were friends in high school, but this is definitely not the boy I used to know. This is a full-grown man with a panty-dropping smile, who could steal your girlfriend and your mama too.

A shrill sound cuts in, and it's almost like nails on a chalkboard. "Mater? Who the hell is Mater?" The nickname is said with such disdain, like it tastes sour coming out of her mouth. Immediately, I want to tell *Blondie* to mind her business and back up out of my conversation. But before I can even say a word, Mason begins to speak.

"That... would be me. Because this girl had a way of making me blush like a tomato when no one else could." If I know Mason as well as I used to, I would say he's blushing right now. "Avery, this is Quinn Parker. Quinn, this is Avery."

With a tight expression on her face, Avery asks, "You know her?" *Seriously, what did I do to this woman? Wait, they aren't...*

"I'm sorry. I didn't realize you two were dating," I say, genuinely apologetic.

Mason is quick to respond. "We are not dating." He seems a bit too emphatic on the word "not" if you asked me, but it's none of my business. "Avery just works here, and I happen to come in pretty frequently with some guys I know." There's a brief flicker of hurt on Avery's face before she quickly recovers. It looks like her feelings are one-sided, and I kind of feel bad for her. With the glow-up Mason has had, I'd imagine women are throwing themselves at him left and right.

I put my hands up in surrender and say, "I didn't mean to imply anything. I just wanted to make sure I wasn't stepping on anyone's toes."

"You aren't stepping on anyone's anything, Quinn. I'm very single and have been for quite some time." *Interesting...* Avery blows out an irritated huff and walks away to take care of some other customers.

I lean into him and quietly say, "I don't know if you know this Mason, but it's obvious that girl is smitten with you. And clearly, she didn't like it when I called you by your nickname." I poke him in the ribs, making him squirm. My touch lingers just a few seconds too long, as I'm momentarily frozen by the feel of his hard muscles underneath my fingertips.

"I know she is, but I've tried as delicately and politely as I can to let her know I'm not interested." He turns on his stool, facing me completely and giving me his full attention. There's a fire burning behind those whiskey-colored orbs as they focus intently on me. He holds my gaze as his tongue peeks out and sweeps his lower lip. "But I *am* interested in someone. Always have been," he says, his tone full of intensity and dominance.

He holds me captive with those beautiful eyes of his, and his honeyed sound practically has me hypnotized.

Whoever this woman is he's interested in, I have the sudden urge to track her down and scratch her eyes out. The flare of jealousy must show on my face, and Mason responds by gently lifting my chin with his index finger.

"No need for that look, Kitten. You already know her." He's never called me "Kitten" before, but the way he practically purrs the word has my belly fluttering with butterflies. I narrow my eyes with an expression of curiosity, as I wonder who it is that has his interest. He leans forward until our lips are just a few inches apart, and I can't help but stare at his full, luscious mouth. *When did Mason Reed become so fucking gorgeous?*

He runs his thumb across my bottom lip, gently tugging it down in a slow move that is both sensual and sexy. My thighs immediately clench as I feel my core begin to tingle. "That girl is you."

THREE

MASON

I can't believe Quinn Parker is here, in one of my favorite bars, sitting one seat away from me.

It's been years since I've seen her, sometime back in college maybe, when we were both home for a school break. But we didn't really get much of a chance to talk then. And now the girl that I've had a crush on since high school is right here in front of me, and this time, I'm not letting her go.

Let's just hope my secret doesn't run her off.

Her gaze is intense as I gently tug her plump lower lip with my thumb. The tiny pink tip of her tongue flicks out and licks my finger, the move causing my dick to twitch. There's mischief in her eyes as a slow smirk spreads across her beautiful face. Still the same flirt, I see. I reach for her hand and give it a slight pull.

"Come over here." My command is confident as I nod my head, signaling for her to sit next to me.

"And you just assume, after all these years, I want to sit with you?" There is that sass I've always loved.

"Are you going to be a brat, Quinn? Or, are you going to do what we both know you want to do and join me for dinner?" She playfully rolls her eyes but slides her menu and drinks down the bar toward me. She gets up from her seat and lifts her coat from the stool between us, laying it on the one she just vacated.

As she sits down, I'm hit with a familiar scent I haven't smelled in almost ten years—fresh summer peaches. The light, sweet fragrance reminds me of the days I used to sit behind her in class, daydreaming about bending her over her desk and fucking her stupid. Even as a teenager, I had these wicked thoughts. I wonder what she'll think now, when she finds out how they've manifested.

She seems a bit nervous, her hands running up and down her thick, denim-covered thighs. I tuck a stray curl behind her ear and lean in to whisper, "What's wrong, Quinn? You haven't gone all shy on me now, have you?" My voice is as smooth as silk before I run my thumb around the shell of her ear. I see her body quiver, and I love knowing how responsive she is to my touch.

Sure, I've touched her before, but it was strictly platonic. As a scrawny kid, I knew I didn't stand a chance with her, no matter how badly I wanted her. Every guy in school wanted to date Quinn, and I'm pretty sure even some of the teachers too. But she seemed to be completely oblivious to her charm and beauty. All I could do was be her friend, and savor every moment I had with her.

She turns to face me, her thighs intertwining with mine. "I don't remember you being so... self-assured back when we were kids."

I give a small chuckle. "It's hard to be self-assured when you're a gawky teenager with acne, who blushes anytime a pretty girl looks his way."

"But I thought you only blushed when I was around. That's why I called you *Mater*." She doesn't realize it, but her sweet mouth slightly puckers into a little pout, making her look so fucking adorable.

"You were the only pretty girl I ever seemed to notice." Now, she's the one blushing. "You know I had a huge crush on you, right?"

Her mouth drops open in a tiny "O" and I envision her on her knees with those sensual, glossy lips wrapped around my cock. The image causes my dick to weep, and I shift in my seat to make room for the steel pipe lengthening in my pants.

She closes her mouth, swallowing hard and blinking those pretty gray-blue eyes, as if clearing the thoughts in her head. "I... I didn't know that."

"You were dating that idiot basketball player. What was his name again?" Of course, I remember his name. Fucking Dave. *Dumbass.* He didn't deserve Quinn, or even a girl like Quinn. I don't know what she was doing with a moron like him.

She shakes her head and blows out a breath. "His name was Dave. And he was a jerk. I definitely stayed with him way longer than I should have. But it was high school, and I was kind of stupid. Obviously." She lifts her shoulders in a small shrug.

"You weren't stupid, Quinn. He just fooled you like he fooled everyone else."

"Well, at least I smartened up and dumped his ass

before we went off to college. And then I proceeded to date a few more losers, before I gave up and focused on school and my career. I guess I'm not really good at picking men, am I?" She scrunches up her little nose, and she looks so damn cute. *Fuck, I've missed her.*

"And somehow, all those losers have led you right here to me. Sorry, not sorry, Quinn." I gently squeeze her knee and her thighs clamp together, showing me she's getting turned on. *Good, that makes two of us.*

"Um, well... that's not exactly how I ended up here. I just got a new job and moved here yesterday. I was supposed to be driving back home for Christmas, but I guess the snow had other plans." I watch as she drops her chin and sadness covers her beautiful face. It hits me right in the chest, and I'd give my left nut to make it go away. Happy Quinn is like fucking sunshine, but sad Quinn is like looking at an injured puppy.

"Yeah, looks like I won't be going home either. I was planning to just hang out in my apartment, but I guess Santa brought my present early." I lift her chin with my index finger, forcing her to look at me as I invade her space. I gaze down at her pillowy soft lips and note that her breaths quicken as I stare at what I'm dying to taste. Lifting my eyes back up to hers, I say, "Looks like you're spending Christmas with me, Quinn Parker."

As I lean toward her sweet mouth, a voice as cold as ice shatters the moment. "Are you gonna order something to eat, or are you gonna stare at Mason all night?" I turn my head to find Avery standing in front of us from behind the bar, an annoyed look on her face with her hands planted haughtily on her hips.

Knowing how fiery Quinn can be—a trait that's always made my dick ache with need—I reply to Avery before Quinn can respond. "She'll have the mushroom Swiss burger and sweet potato fries." I push her closed menu toward Avery and give her a hard look, daring her to smart off to Quinn again. She snatches up the menu with a roll of her eyes and a "whatever" huffed under her breath. Turning on her heel, she stomps off to the kitchen without a backward glance, and I refocus my attention on the girl who's had my heart since the 9th grade.

I'm going to spend Christmas with Quinn Parker. And the best present ever—I hope—will be this gorgeous girl tied to my bed while I fuck her relentlessly. I want her to know how I've felt about her over the years. And I hope she can accept that the Mater she once knew is all grown up and comes with some new kinks.

FOUR

QUINN

"After all this time, you still remember what I like to eat?" I'm trying to wrap my head around how he knows what to order for me. And the fact that he just took control of the situation and *did it*. If it were anyone else, I wouldn't stand for a man being so high-handed. But with Mason, I find his confidence hot as hell.

"Do you not remember how many Friday-night meals we shared at the diner after all the football games? You'd be so hungry after cheering the whole game that you'd still be in your uniform while you ate the same meal every week."

"Oh yeah! You'd always wait for me after the home games, so we could meet up with everybody at Sunny's. I didn't realize you paid attention to what I was eating though."

"I paid attention to everything you did, Quinn. It was hard not to." Just knowing that Mason had his eyes on me, even back then, causes a little tingle in my belly as a soft blush heats my cheeks.

21

We continue to catch up, and it isn't long before my food is brought out and I join Mason in eating dinner. Talking with him feels so good and reminds me of home, so much so, I momentarily forget I'm disappointed about my ruined plans.

As we're eating and talking and laughing, I see an extremely attractive man, with his hair cut low into a perfect fade with deep waves, headed our way. When he gets closer, I take in his megawatt smile with straight white teeth, a well-trimmed beard covering his milk chocolate complexion, and dark eyes the color of espresso that twinkle with mischief. Whoever this man is, I have no doubt he leaves a wake of broken hearts wherever he goes.

"Mason!" the man draws out as he stands behind him, clapping his hands down on his shoulders. He winks at me just as Mason turns on his stool to face the new arrival.

"Tommy. Hey, man, I thought you were headed outta town. What are you doing here?" Mason's voice has taken on a bit of a cooler tone, like he's annoyed this guy came over.

"Eh, change of plans. You know, with the weather." Tommy looks in my direction and doesn't hide his perusal as his eyes skim up and down my body. I'm sure this guy is charming to some, but for whatever reason, I'm not sure I like the way he's eyeing me. Mason's gaze sharpens when he notices Tommy checking me out.

"Mase, man. Aren't you gonna introduce me to your pretty friend?"

It's clear Mason doesn't want to, but he decides to be

polite anyway. "Tommy, this is Quinn. Quinn, this is Tommy. He and I work together." Mason doesn't offer any more information, and it's obvious he wants him to go away, but Tommy doesn't catch on.

Extending my hand, I reach out to Tommy expecting a handshake. Instead, he turns it over and brings my knuckles to his lips for a kiss. "Quinn. That's a beautiful name for a beautiful woman. How do you know our Mason here?" He's still holding on to me as he speaks, so I tug my hand back and place it in my lap.

Mason lays his palm on my thigh in a possessive gesture before answering for me. "Quinn and I went to high school together. She just moved here for work." He gives me a sexy smile and gently squeezes my leg, which unexpectedly makes my pussy flutter.

"Ah, new to the city then. I'd be happy to show you around sometime. Take you to all the cool places to hang out, the best food spots... Show you what our city has to offer." It's obvious he means what *he* has to offer.

I begin to respond, "Well, I—" but Mason answers at the same time.

Flashing a sly smirk, Mason says, "That's so nice of you to offer, Tommy, but Quinn and I already have plans. There're lots of things I'm gonna show her." Mason's warm palm runs up and down my thigh, and it's clear he's letting Tommy know to back off. Tommy's eyes catch the movement, then flicker between me and Mason. The heat in his gaze quickly cools as he picks up on Mason's unspoken claim. *When did that happen?*

"I see. Well, if you decide you want a different tour guide, you just let me know." *Don't worry, I won't.* A low growl escapes from Mason's throat as he gives Tommy a scathing look. Tommy's eyes widen in surprise for just a moment, before he quickly schools his expression and turns the charm back on.

"It was nice meeting you, Quinn. I'll see you at the office next week, Mase. Merry Christmas." He gives Mason a lift of his chin before patting him on the back and hastily walking away, his tail tucked as he goes.

I pivot to Mason with a bit of shock and awe, and ask, "Who are you? What did you do with the shy Mater?"

"Mater grew up, babe. And now he takes what's his." This possessive, dominating man sitting in front of me is a vast contrast to the sweet boy I grew up with. And it's seriously turning me on.

THROUGH THE COURSE OF OUR MEAL, WE DISCOVER MASON and I both live in the same apartment building down the street, and he resides just two floors above me. We finish our food and a few more drinks before deciding to call it a night. I'm having such an amazing time being with him again, until it's time to go home and I remember I'm still bummed.

"Why the sad face, Kitten?" There's that endearment again that makes my thighs clench.

"Just thinking about not seeing my parents for the holidays."

"I'm sorry, Quinn." Mason tucks a curl behind my ear as he thoughtfully looks into my eyes. "Let's get you home. I've got a few things I need to do tonight."

By "things" I kind of hope he means *me*, but that would be weird, right? We haven't seen each other in years. But somehow, it feels like we haven't been apart at all. We've just picked right back up where we left off as friends, but now, I want it to turn into more.

Mason pays our tab after refusing to let me pay my half. We bundle up in our coats and gloves, and head out into the cold night air. I loop my arm through his and rest my head on his broad shoulder, as we walk the short distance to our apartment building.

"Just like old times, huh, Mater?"

"Yeah. But a lot's changed since then, Quinn."

"I see that," I say as I playfully squeeze his bulging bicep. "My little Mater has turned into quite the hottie." I can't believe I'm flirting with Mason Reed. *But a girl's gotta do what a girl's gotta do.*

"That's not all that's changed, Quinn. But we'll talk about that later." He gives me a devilish grin, and I must say I'm intrigued to know what he means by that.

We get to my floor and he insists on walking me to my front door. I fish for my keys in my coat pocket and he takes them from my hand, unlocking the door for me. Always such a gentleman.

I decide to be brave and ask, "Do you... wanna come inside? We can catch up some more." Nerves dance in my belly as I worry my lower lip between my teeth.

Mason gently tugs my lip free with his thumb, then slowly slides it back and forth across my plump flesh. "I can't tonight. I have some things I need to take care of." He must read the disappointment on my face, because he says, "Don't be upset with me, Kitten."

"Oh, I'm not upset. It's totally fine. I'm sure you're busy." I try my best to play it off and dip my head so he can't see my embarrassment.

He lifts my chin with his forefinger. "I'm never too busy for you, Quinn. And I meant it when I said you're mine for Christmas." When he says "mine" in that deep, rich voice of his, my heart stutters a few beats.

"Be ready by 8 a.m. tomorrow morning. I'll come down to pick you up. And pack an overnight bag." There's a flicker in his eyes, and I know he's up to something.

"What are you planning, Mason?" My forehead wrinkles as I cock my head in curiosity.

"You'll see, Kitten. Just be ready. I know you won't disappoint me."

"And if I do?" My left brow rises as I ask the question.

"Are you being a brat again? I'll have to show you my preferred way of handling brats." Heat flashes in his gaze, and I can tell he likes the little game we're playing. "Behave, Quinn. And be ready for me tomorrow morning."

He leans in and kisses my cheek, his lips pressing against my skin just a little longer than necessary. His clean, masculine cologne fills my nose as I feel the heat from his body radiating off him. Dear God, I'll do anything this man asks me to.

"Good night, Kitten. I'll see you in the morning."

"Why do you call me *Kitten*?"

"I'll tell you tomorrow. Now, go inside and lock up for me. Tomorrow's Christmas Eve and I have plans for you."

Before I can kiss him good night, he nudges me inside

and pulls the door closed behind me. I turn the deadbolt, then rise on my tiptoes to peek through the peephole.

Mason rests his hand on the door, a look of longing on his face. He closes his eyes for just a moment, before stuffing his hands in his coat pockets and heading back to the elevator.

Mason Reed is here with me. And we're spending the holiday together. This might not be such a bad Christmas after all.

FIVE

MASON

Walking away from Quinn was so much harder than I made it look. I wanted nothing more than to follow her sweet ass inside her apartment and crush my mouth to hers in a searing kiss. But the time isn't right just yet, and I need to make sure she's okay with what I have in store for her.

I know this is the first time she's spent Christmas away from her family, so I'm going to do everything I can to make it good for her. More than that, she deserves to have somebody going out of their way to take care of her. After everything she told me at dinner tonight, it's clear that Quinn thinks of everyone else around her but never herself. The whole time she was talking, the same question played on repeat in my head: *who is taking care of this beautiful girl?*

Well, I know who's taking care of her now, and that's going to be me. I did my best to be there for her when we were in high school, but I can damn sure do a much better job of it now. And I know exactly how to start.

I pull my phone from my pocket and make a quick call. I know just the right person, someone who will tell me exactly what I need to do. After two rings, the call connects and a familiar sound comes across the line.

"Hi, honey! How's my sweet boy?"

"Mom, I haven't been a boy in quite some time." I chuckle softly at the ridiculous thought that my mom still sees me as a kid.

"You'll always be my sweet boy, no matter how old you are. Now, to what do I owe the pleasure of this call? Because I just talked to you a few hours ago."

"You did, but something's come up, and I need your help."

"Oh? What's that?"

"Do you remember Quinn Parker? From high school? She was a cheerleader in my class."

"The girl you were obsessed with?" There's a teasing tone to my mother's voice, but also an undertone that dares me to prove her wrong.

"I wasn't obsessed with her, Mom. We were just friends. That's all."

"She may have been just your friend, but it was obvious you were smitten with her." *Shit, was it?*

"How was it obvious?"

"Oh, Mason. I'm your mother. I know when my son has the hots for a girl."

"I didn't have the hots for her," I deadpan. "And no one says that anymore, Mom."

"Well, whatever you kids call it. I just know it was obvious to me and everyone else that you liked her. Anyway, what does this have to do with your call?"

There's hope in my mom's voice, and I can tell she's getting excited. She's been after me to find a "good girl to settle down with" for years now. But there's only ever been one girl I wanted to do that with, and now's my chance.

"As it turns out, Quinn is here, in the city with me. And we're both stuck because of the snow. We're gonna spend the holiday together, and I really wanna make it special for her. This is her first time being away from home for Christmas." I think about Quinn's sad face every time she remembered that she wasn't going home to be with her parents. I know that whatever it takes, I'm going to make sure this is a holiday she doesn't forget.

"Aww, see! You *are* a sweet boy!" I can't help the roll of my eyes as I hear my mom clap her hands in excitement.

"So... suggestions here?"

For the next 10 minutes, I listen as Mom gives me a laundry list of things to do for Quinn. I know she's spot on with her ideas, and Quinn is going to love it.

I wrap up the call with my mom and tell her I'll talk to her tomorrow for Christmas Eve. I do a quick supply check of the items I have on hand prior to making a list of things I need to get from the store. I put my coat and gloves back on, before picking up my keys from the ceramic bowl on the entryway table by the door. Checking my watch, I see I have just enough time to make it before the store closes. I can't wait to see Quinn's face when she finds out what I'm doing for her.

TRYING TO GO TO SLEEP WITH THE WORLD'S HARDEST DICK is definitely proving to be a challenge. As I lie here in my bed, anticipating spending time with Quinn tomorrow, my dick just keeps getting harder and harder. It was always this way anytime I thought of her, even all those years ago. She probably thought I had some kind of deformity, since I spent most of our high school years walking awkwardly, trying to hide the raging boner I had whenever she was near me.

God, she's so fucking beautiful, and she doesn't even know it.

Those lush, soft curls. Her smooth, clear skin. And that curvy body that could only be made for sin... And that fucking mouth. I dare someone to find a more perfect pair of lips made just right to wrap around my dick.

Before I even realize what I'm doing, I free my long, thick cock from my boxer briefs and begin tugging it in smooth, fluid strokes. Precum starts to drip from the tip, and I gather it in my palm to use as lube. My head falls back as I begin to fuck my hand, imagining Quinn's eyes are on me while sucking me deep into her hot, wet mouth.

I squeeze the full head of my dick with each upward stroke, my heavy sac beginning to tighten up. Dreaming of her being here with me, submitting completely to me and my every fantasy, only makes me stroke my dick faster and harder.

It's throbbing now, as the thick vein that runs underneath pulses with the need to come. There's a tingle at the base of my spine as my balls draw up even more. It doesn't take much longer before I blow my load and cum spurts out all over my hand and abs.

This isn't the first time I've jerked off to thoughts of Quinn Parker. But the next time I do, it won't be to the fantasy of her. Because the next time a hand is on my dick, I'm going to make damn sure it's hers.

SIX

QUINN

There's excitement stirring in my belly as I flit around my apartment, tearing through boxes and gathering things I need for the day with Mason. When I got home last night, I was a little bummed that he had something else to do and couldn't stay. But what could I expect after suddenly running into him after all these years? That he either had no plans or that he'd drop them just for me, a girl he hadn't seen since college? *Yeah, not likely.*

Still, it didn't keep me from wishing for something different. And it certainly didn't keep me from giving myself two orgasms, as I thought about all the wicked things he could do to me with that sexy-as-fuck body of his.

It's actually kind of strange to think of Mason this way, because I didn't see him like this back when we were friends. Sure, I thought he was super cute in high school, but it was strictly platonic. He was safe, and I felt one hundred percent confident that I could tell him anything and he wouldn't judge me for it. The truth is he probably knows me better than anyone else, and that's not something I take lightly.

I still remember the first day of freshman geometry when I was running late and plopped down at my desk just seconds before the bell. Mason was already seated at the desk behind mine, patiently waiting for class to begin.

I frantically pulled my notebook and pen out of my backpack, paying absolutely no mind to what was going on around me. Mason was trying to get my attention to pass me a stack of handouts that were circulating the room. I turned in my chair just as his hand was coming around my side, and before I could register what was happening, I knocked all the papers to the floor.

I quickly bent down to pick them up at the exact same time as Mason. And just like some kind of romance novel meet-cute, we bumped heads, causing us both to break out in a fit of laughter. I'm sure I looked like a bumbling idiot, and I probably should've been embarrassed. But instead, Mason just smiled at me warmly and made me forget all about my clumsiness.

That's what he does for me—he makes me feel safe to just be me. There's never any judgment or criticism, just respect, and care, and kindness. He was always there to listen to me, no matter what I was talking about. And when I needed someone to cheer me on or listen to me whine, or even be a shoulder to cry on, he was always there for me.

It broke my heart when he told me he was going out of state for college, but I understood he needed to go to the school that had the best program for his major. After that, life just got busy and we kind of fell out of touch. But there wasn't a single day that went by that I didn't think of him or wonder what he was up to. I'm hoping now is our chance to make up for lost time.

I check my cell phone to see what time it is, just as three sharp knocks rap on the door. Using my phone's camera, I hurriedly look over my appearance before pocketing the device and crossing the room to answer the door. After unlocking the deadbolt and removing the chain, I open the door to reveal the sexiest man I've ever seen, dressed in red and black buffalo plaid sleep pants and a tight black waffle-knit thermal shirt.

Mason's hair is perfectly tousled and the tanned skin of his hard pecs peeks out from the unbuttoned top of his shirt. His sleeves are pushed up, showcasing the veins in his muscular forearms that have a light dusting of dark hair. If I look closely, I can just discern the multiple firm pillows that make up his eight-pack abs. *It's hot enough in here to melt the damn snow!*

"Are you gonna let me in, or are you gonna stand there and keep eye-fucking me?" My eyes snap up to his and I observe his ridiculously sexy grin. Thoroughly embarrassed, my neck and face flame with shame over being caught for blatantly gawking at his glorious body. Unable to speak, I move to the side to allow him to enter while I try to find my tongue.

Mason walks in like he owns the damn place, and I must admit the swagger he now has is hot as hell. He surveys the room with an air of confidence before turning around and taking in my appearance. His gaze slowly drifts up and down my body, then he shakes his head and tsks his tongue at me.

"You can't wear that today."

I looked down at my clothes, then back at him with a puzzled expression on my face. "What's wrong with what I have on?"

"You look beautiful, Kitten, but it's Christmas Eve. We're going to be hanging out in my apartment and lounging all day. You can't be relaxed in skinny jeans and a sweater."

"Oh. Well, I wasn't exactly sure what we were doing today, so I didn't wanna show up looking like a bum in my pajamas." My fingers nervously tug at the hem of my pink cashmere sweater. Mason closes the distance between us and grabs my hands, halting my fidgeting.

"I have a big day planned for us, but you won't be leaving my apartment anytime soon." Heat and lust flash in his eyes as butterflies dance in my belly. "Go change into something comfortable. Something... soft. I'll wait out here for you."

He squeezes my hands gently before releasing my wrists and nudging me in the direction of my bedroom. As I walk past him, he swiftly smacks my ass, which causes me to jump and bite my lower lip. When I turn back to look at him over my shoulder, he gives me a smoldering grin. I swiftly make my way to my room and change into something more comfortable, wanting to see that sexy smirk again as soon as possible.

I don my favorite black yoga pants and a red racer-back tank with a picture of Santa on the front, above black text that says: *There're some hoes in this house.*

Smiling at the ridiculous shirt I found online, I promptly make my way back to the living room. As soon as Mason sees my shirt, he shakes his head and chuckles.

"I don't know why I would expect anything different from you, Quinn. That shirt fits you perfectly." I give him a flirty wink.

"C'mon, Mater. Take me to your place."

"My fucking pleasure, Kitten. Let's go."

SEVEN

MASON

I help Quinn slip on a black zip-up hoodie before grabbing her packed weekender bag that's next to the front door. After ensuring her apartment is all locked up, I link her fingers with mine and tug her behind me down the hallway.

I look over my shoulder as we're walking toward the elevator and catch the soft blush coloring her cheeks. I shoot her a wink and her blush deepens. The fact that I can affect her like this only makes my dick twitch, dying to get close to her.

When we get to my place, I unlock the door and open it wide, gesturing for her to walk in ahead of me. After locking up behind us and setting her bag down on the floor, I turn to reach for her, but she's already gone. Quinn has taken it upon herself to explore my apartment, and seeing her here in a place that I rarely allow anyone to see has my chest filling with warmth.

Our apartments are basically the same layout, but mine is in reverse, since it's on the other side of the hallway. I watch as she walks over to the slim Christmas tree I have minimally decorated by the large window in my living room. Her long, slender fingers reach out to touch the red and green ornaments hanging on the branches, before she turns and eyes me inquisitively.

"This looks new, like it's right out of the box."

Stuffing my hands in my pockets, I respond to her observation. "It is. I'm not big on Christmas, so I don't ever decorate. Nothing against the holiday, I'm just usually back home with my family, so I don't see the point of putting up decorations that I won't be here to enjoy." The furrow in her brow deepens.

"So, you went out and bought a tree at the last minute?"

"For you, Quinn. I wanted it to still feel like Christmas for you." Her face relaxes as her hand comes up to rest at the top of her chest.

"I'd almost forgotten how incredibly sweet you are. You didn't have to do this, Mason."

"It was nothing. C'mon. Let's get you some breakfast. I'm starving." I take her hand and lead her over to the kitchen, pulling out a barstool from the breakfast counter. She climbs onto the seat as her eyes widen, taking in the spread of food in front of her.

"Is this all for me?" The expression of awe and excitement on her face is adorable.

"It's for me too, so I hope you plan on sharing." I made her favorite breakfast of fluffy French toast with warm maple syrup, thick-cut bacon, sausage, scrambled eggs with cheese, and fresh-squeezed orange juice. And, yeah, I really did squeeze a shit-ton of oranges to make a full carafe of juice just for her.

"I... this looks amazing!" She peers up at me like I just hung the moon, and I vow right now that I'll do whatever it takes to see that look on her face every day for the rest of my life.

"I promised to give you a great holiday, Kitten. I figured it couldn't hurt to start off with your favorite breakfast."

She hops down from her stool and comes around the counter to give me a big bear hug. She presses every inch of her curvy body against mine as her long arms wrap tightly around my waist. Quinn rests her head on my chest, and the scent of her coconut shampoo fills my nose as I bend down to kiss her crown of dark hair.

I close my eyes and savor every second of her embrace. As I get lost in her touch, my dick chooses that moment to wake up, nudging her lower belly and seeking attention.

I should be a gentleman and pull away from her, but I don't. I want her to know exactly what she does to me. I hid my feelings from her all through school, and I'm done with that. I have another chance with Quinn, and this time, I'm taking it.

I know the precise moment she notices my hardening dick, because I hear a small gasp leave her lips. She starts to pull away, but I hold on tighter, keeping her from escaping. Just as I begin to question if I'm making her uncomfortable, she presses into me and I feel her smile against my chest. *Naughty fucking girl.*

"Behave, Kitten, and eat your breakfast." Reluctantly, I release her and spin her back in the direction of her seat.

"I didn't start it, sir." Her smirk barely registers, since my brain seems to be stuck on her calling me *sir*. I really like the sound of it coming from her luscious mouth.

"Technically, my dick started it," I say as I discreetly try to adjust my hard cock, which is extremely visible through my thin flannel pajama pants.

"Semantics." She cocks her brow at me as she slides onto her stool.

We both pile our plates high, eating our food while having a relaxed conversation. I've enjoyed reminiscing with her, but not as much as I've loved getting to know her as the "grown-up" Quinn, and not just the gorgeous cheerleader I used to pine after.

After breakfast, she insists on helping me clean up the kitchen and notices the two reusable grocery bags I have sitting next to my pantry. She takes a step in the direction of the bags, and I move in front of her to block her path.

"What's that you're hiding over there?" She peers around my body, rising on her tiptoes while trying to steal a better look.

"It's for later." I offer nothing more as she drops back down on her heels, giving me a small pout of her lips. "That pout won't work on me, Quinn," I tell her as I bop the tip of her cute nose with my index finger.

"It used to work all the time... Mater." Her eyes sparkle with sass, knowing that I know she's right. I'm not going to tell her it still works, because I really want her surprises coming all day.

"Let's get outta the kitchen so you won't be tempted to peek. I have your favorite movie cued up and ready to go."

"Fiiiiiine." She drags out the word, rolling her eyes at me playfully while letting me take her hand, as I guide her back to the living room. But just as we reach the couch, she stops me.

"Wait. I want the rest of the tour first."

"My apartment is the same as yours, Quinn. There's nothing much to see."

"I want to see your bedroom. I bet that's different from mine."

"And just what do you think you'll learn from seeing my bedroom?"

"You can learn a lot about a person from their bedroom. Their private space. The room that, in theory, only a select few get to see."

I hesitate for just a minute, knowing what I'm hiding from her is locked up in that room. But she won't know what it is just from a quick glance around my space. I need a little bit more time with her before I reveal my secret.

Grudgingly, I give in to her. "Okay, but let's make it quick. There's not much to see in there, and I wanna watch this movie with you."

Before I can guide her down the hall, she gives a little victory dance and darts off ahead of me. She doesn't even look back to see if I've followed and barges straight into my bedroom. I catch up to her just as she flicks on the light and begins looking around.

I squirm a little bit under her observing eyes,

knowing she's taking in every detail of my private space. The decor is very masculine with warm, rich, dark colors. But the space still feels comforting and inviting with soft touches added, like a throw blanket and decorative pillows on the bed and the oversized chair by the window.

She stops next to the large padded chest at the end of my bed. To most people, it just looks like a normal bench that you'd find in any bedroom. But this one comes with a lock keeping it shut and away from prying eyes. I hold my breath, anticipating what's about to happen, but she surprises me and continues looking around the room.

"I love your bed! It's so... unique." She glides her long fingers along the edge of the headboard, taking in the mix of steel and wood.

"It's an exclusive design. Something I had custom-made just for me." I covertly toy with one of the hidden rings that's built into the footboard. My gaze flicks up and I find her watching me, curiosity dancing in her eyes.

"Too good for just any old bed from the furniture store, are we?" she teases me.

"Not at all. I just needed something that was a little better suited for my... particular tastes."

"I didn't know you were so particular, Mason."

"Very." My eyes roam all over her hot little body and my cock begins to twitch. "Have you seen enough yet?" We need to get out of this room, before I throw her on the bed and show her just what I've been up to all these years.

"For now," she says nonchalantly as the corner of her mouth turns up slightly. She walks toward me, her curvy hips swaying in her tight black yoga pants. Her mouth-watering tits are barely covered by her graphic tank. Fuck me, she's gorgeous.

As she gets closer, I see a glimmer of heat in her eyes. Just as I think she's about to put her hands on me, she turns slightly to the side and walks out of my room. It's only then that I realized I was holding my breath.

EIGHT

QUINN

He's hiding something in that room, and I know it. *But what?*

He lives alone, so why the big lock on the chest at the end of his bed? I know he's not securing sweaters and blankets in there. And even if it were keepsakes and heirlooms, I can't imagine that they would need to be kept under lock and key in his own apartment.

Maybe he's Batman. I giggle at my own ridiculousness.

"What's so funny?" Mason asks as he follows me to the couch.

"It's nothing. Don't pay me any attention." I melt into his amazingly comfortable couch, pulling a fluffy fleece blanket over my legs. "What's this movie you've got lined up for us?"

"Movies. Plural." Mason joins me, stealing half of the blanket and forcing me to scoot closer to him. Our thighs touch and a zip of electricity shoots through my core. "We'll watch *Christmas Vacation* first, then your next surprise, and then *Scrooged*."

"So, you really were listening to me talk last night, weren't you?" I give him a teasing poke in the ribs.

"I pay attention when you talk, Quinn. And I definitely take note of the important things like your favorite movies."

"Wait, you mentioned my next surprise. Well, what is it?" My eyebrows rise in excitement.

"It wouldn't be a surprise if I told you, now, would it? Be patient, Kitten."

I exhale an exasperated huff. "Fine, start the damn movie." Mason chuckles as he turns on the TV, the movie cued up and ready to play.

He nudges a little closer, putting his arm around me in a warm cuddle. I breathe in the scent of his spicy, woodsy body wash mixed with the smell of his heated skin. I close my eyes, resisting the urge to crawl into his lap and let him hold me.

I have no doubt if I did just that, he would wrap me up in a tight embrace. But it's not just snuggling I'm after. I want what I didn't get all those years ago. What I didn't realize was right in front of me, because I was dating that idiot, Dave.

I want the man who looks like a fucking romance book cover model. The man with tousled dark hair and whiskey-colored eyes and bulging, corded muscles under smooth, golden skin. The man that I'm sure wants me just as much as I want him.

But he's keeping a secret from me. And he's slow-playing me. I'll allow it for now, but he's going to have to come clean sooner rather than later.

IT TURNS OUT MASON'S SECOND SURPRISE WAS MAKING sugar cookies. The two bags sitting by the pantry contained all the ingredients to make them from scratch, as well as various cookie cutters, sprinkles, and colored icings. This man is trying to kill me with his sweetness— my favorite breakfast, my favorite movies, and now my favorite Christmas cookies. If he brings out peppermint hot chocolate, my heart is going to explode from swooning.

We're watching *Die Hard*, another holiday favorite of mine, while lazing around on the couch. Mason excused himself a few minutes ago, and I took the opportunity to move the huge plate of cookies into my lap. Taking a big bite of a frosted, sugary snowman, I close my eyes, relishing the delicious goodness.

"Need something to wash that down?" My eyes pop open, and I turn my head in the direction of Mason's voice, which I hear coming from right behind me.

Annnnnd time of death? 6:17 p.m.

Mason walks toward me from the kitchen, carrying two steaming reindeer mugs. I can smell the peppermint wafting through the room, and I know right away he's bringing me hot chocolate. This man is just too damn perfect.

"Here, Kitten. Your favorite Christmas Eve drink."

"How are you this incredible and still single?" I take the offered mug from his hands and look at him in complete wonderment.

"Because I've been waiting for the right girl." My eyes

slightly widen, questioning his implication. He shakes his head and says, "I'm not a monk, Quinn. I just haven't found anyone I wanted to be serious with. I'm pretty sure I'm finally realizing now why that is."

"Because..." My body mindlessly leans toward him with hope.

"Because of you, Kitten. I realize now it's all because of you. No one could ever compare to you and no one ever will."

He looks deeply into my eyes, holding me captive with his stare. There's a myriad of emotions crossing his face before finally landing on what I think might be love. But that's impossible. He can't just love me after one day.

"Who said it was just one day?" Fuck. I realize I said that out loud and dip my head in embarrassment, as heat creeps up my cheeks. He grips my chin and forces me to look at him, and I'm mesmerized by what I see there.

We gaze at each other for several beats, before I ask, "Why do you call me *Kitten*?"

Without breaking his stare, he responds, "Because you can be cute and cuddly, but you're also fierce with sharp claws. You're smart, cunning, and no one sees you coming until you pounce.

"You're extremely independent and don't need anyone to give you what you need, but that doesn't mean you don't want them to. Without intentionally doing it, you make people crave your attention, but you're selective of whom receives it—making the person who does get it feel like they're someone important, someone... special."

I foolishly thought it was just some generic nickname, but now I see it's so much more than that, and it makes me feel like a queen. Part of me is embarrassed by his appraisal, but the other part of me wants to preen like the kitten he thinks I am.

"And you just realized these things about me?"

"No, Quinn. These are things I've always known about you. And I've called you *Kitten* in my head since we were in school. It's only now that I'm able to say it to you out loud."

"Why now?"

"Because I missed out on you before, and I'm not gonna let that happen again." He lightly grips the hand resting on my thigh and rubs slow circles on the back of it with his thumb. "But I do need to tell you something. And honestly, I'm really not sure how you're going to react."

Trepidation is written all over his gorgeous face as a sense of foreboding creeps into the room. I have no idea what he's about to say, but I'm suddenly filled with nervousness as my flight response wants to kick in.

Has he been buttering me up all day, just to hit me with bad news? *Dammit, I knew it had to be too good to be true.*

NINE

MASON

My stomach knots up as I think about Quinn rejecting me and what I'm about to tell her. When I've shared this side of me with others in the past, it's mostly been met with a mix of curiosity, outright fear, and even disgust. If Quinn and I are really meant to be, then how she responds to my secret will let me know for sure.

She pulls her hand back from underneath mine, before lifting the plate of cookies off her lap and placing it on the coffee table. She turns in her seat to face me fully, giving me her complete attention. I take in her beautiful face as I hear her swallow loudly, looking at me as if I'm about to tell her something that's going to break her heart. But it's not her heart I'm worried about; it's mine.

"I think we should have this conversation in my bedroom." I stand, offering her my hand to help her up while praying she takes it and doesn't run.

"I don't see how that's going to make this conversation

any easier for either one of us," she says softly, her voice filled with apprehension.

"It will; you'll see. Will you please come with me?" If she turns me down, I know it's for the best. If she can't trust me right now, then she's never going to trust me after what I have to show her. And I have to have her complete trust if this is going to work.

Without saying another word, she places her hand in mine and allows me to help her off the couch. I let out a breath I didn't know I was holding and give her palm a gentle squeeze. Without letting go, I tug her behind me as we silently head to my bedroom. Once inside, I walk her to my bed and seat her on the edge as I remain standing.

Where the fuck do I even start?

I take a few deep breaths as I pace the floor in front of her. While I'm mulling over my options, my thoughts are disrupted when I hear her voice.

"Can you sit down? You're kinda freaking me out a little bit."

I don't say anything, but I stop pacing and sit down next to her. Maybe this will be easier to say if I'm not looking directly at her.

"Does this have something to do with the locked chest at the end of your bed?" Of course, she noticed the lock when she was in here earlier.

"It does."

"Would it be easier if you just opened it and let me see what's inside first?" *Fuck, I don't know.* She might take one look and go running for the door. Maybe I should lock the door, just in case. Shaking away the absurd thought I briefly had about holding her captive, I stand again and step in front of her.

If she were anyone else, I really wouldn't care how she reacted. In the past, if someone didn't like this part about me, it didn't really matter, because they weren't someone I wanted to be with long-term anyway. But Quinn has the ability to break me, and she doesn't even know it. If she can't accept this part of me, then I'm pretty sure I'll be alone forever.

"C'mere, Kitten." I reach for her hand and we walk to the foot of the bed. "I'm gonna show you what's inside, but I'm begging you not to run. Please just give me the chance to explain before you say or do anything." Her answer isn't verbal, just a sharp nod of her head as she worries her hands in front of her.

Taking a deep breath, I bend down and twist the numbers on the combination lock. Once the correct six digits are displayed and I can open it, I release the shackle and lift up the padded top of the chest. I already know what Quinn will see, and my heart beats faster anticipating her reaction. When I don't hear anything for a few seconds—other than the blood rushing through my ears—I stand and turn to face her. What I find when I seek her gray-blue eyes shocks the absolute hell out of me, and nothing could've prepared me for it.

QUINN

I have no idea what Mason is hiding from me, but my nerves are through the roof right now. Sitting here on the side of his bed, watching him pace back and forth, has me a little on edge. He makes it seem like I should be terrified of what he's about to say.

In an effort to calm his mind, I offer, "Would it be easier if you just opened it and let me see what's inside first?" He takes a minute to consider what I've said before extending his outstretched hand to me. I take it, and follow him around the bed to stand in front of the locked chest.

I'm pretty sure he's no caped hero, so just what in the hell is he keeping in there? Maybe it's body parts that he's preserved in jars. Nah, he's not giving me serial killer vibes.

Maybe he has some weird doll collection, and he likes to display them when he's alone. If that's the case, I'm out. Their creepy little eyes always seem to follow you around the room and that's freaky as shit.

Or maybe he has some strange celebrity obsession, and he has a bunch of memorabilia he's bought online and things he's found in their trash. *Okay, Quinn. You're being stupid right now. Just stop it.*

I internally roll my eyes at myself for being so ridiculous, and take a deep breath to settle my nerves. Mason reaches down and opens the lock, lifting the top of the chest to show me its contents.

I must say this isn't at all what I expected. And I'm quite relieved at what I see inside. Honestly, I'm pretty fucking happy right now, and I know without a doubt that Mason and I are meant to be together.

As ideas and fantasies begin playing in my head, I can't help the huge smile that spreads across my face. Mason slowly rises from his crouched position and takes a breath as he prepares to see my reaction.

When he turns around and finds me smiling ear to ear, his jaw practically drops to the floor. He looks like a guppy as he opens and closes his mouth a few times, causing me to release a small giggle.

"You're smiling. You're actually fucking smiling." The disbelief in his voice is quite evident.

"I guess you expected a different reaction."

"Fuck yeah, I did. Not many people know what I'm into, but as soon as they find out, most of them act disgusted or afraid, and then they bolt."

"Disgusted? I get it if it's not your jam, but why would they be disgusted?" I cock my head, trying to understand the kind of reaction he describes.

"Because they don't understand the lifestyle and think it's just some weird deviant shit." *Ah. Gotta love those kink shamers.* I shake my head in annoyance.

"I can get someone being trepidatious about it, but it's not deviant or sick." Mason is still looking at me in awe, like I'm a unicorn standing in front of him. "But I do have one question for you though."

He hesitates for a brief moment before nodding his head, encouraging me to continue. I take my time, knowing the anticipation is making him squirm, and I can't help but find a tiny bit of enjoyment in that. I sober my expression and dip my head, needing just a few seconds to contain my laughter. I look up at him through my thick, dark lashes, giving him my best doe eyes, and finally ask my question.

With a very serious tone, I inquire, "Would you prefer a formal or informal binding tonight?" The corners of my lips tip up slowly into a grin. His eyes widen slightly, and I see the exact moment he recognizes from my words that I'm no stranger to what he's been keeping hidden about himself. He doesn't respond to my question, but instead takes my mouth in a punishing kiss, tackling me to the bed.

Looks like Mason Reed and I share the same kink. This is gonna be the naughtiest Christmas I've ever had.

TEN

MASON

She's a rope bunny. Quinn Parker is a fucking rope bunny.
As soon as she asked me about the type of binding I preferred, I knew this girl was meant to be mine. I've wanted her since the first day I laid eyes on her as a freshman. And now, not only do I get to have her, but she shares my appreciation and love of rope.

I will never fucking let her go.

Consumed with elation and heat, I take her down to the mattress, desperately kissing her. My lips press tightly against hers when she opens her mouth, allowing me inside. Her natural flavor mixes with the sweet taste of sugar cookies as my tongue massages hers slowly, passionately.

I turn, positioning us on our sides, so I don't crush her with my weight. After sliding my knee between her thicc thighs, I'm rewarded with a moan and the heat of her pussy as she rolls her hips, seeking the friction she needs. My hands caress the curves of her face when she clasps my wrists and slows my actions.

Between kisses, she breathily says, "You didn't answer my question, Mason. Tell me how you want to bind me tonight." Her words are hushed, her voice laced with desire. With her hands still wrapped around me, I go back in for another kiss before responding.

"As much as I want a formal binding, there's too much to discuss for a proper scene." My dick aches as I envision doing floor work with Quinn, wrapping her in yards of rope, restraining her in different poses. "But I simply don't have the fucking patience tonight. I've wanted you for almost half my life, Quinn. And I need to get inside you as soon as possible."

I attack her mouth again, needing another hit of her sweet taste. I slightly raise my knee, my muscular thigh grinding against her pussy. A soft mewl escapes from her, the sound going straight to my dick, causing it to harden like solid granite. Fuck, I want her so damn bad.

When we both have to break the kiss and come up for air, she asks, "I guess our first time will be vanilla, then?" There's a bratty smirk on her face and I know there was a challenge in her question.

"Now, that wouldn't be the right way to start off our relationship, would it?" I grip her hips and pull her body into mine, rubbing my hard cock against her lower belly. I lean into her and whisper, "Just because we haven't discussed how our formal scenes will go, doesn't mean you won't be tangled up in my ropes tonight." A shiver rolls down her body and her nipples tighten against my chest. I love how quickly she responds to my words.

She rests her forehead against mine and looks deep

into my eyes. "I trust you, Mason. I always have. You have my consent to do whatever you think I'll like... Whatever you think we'll both like." *God, she's perfect.* "Now, go pick out some rope so we can play."

AFTER SEVERAL MINUTES OF KISSING QUINN LIKE MY LIFE depends on it, I force myself to break away from her mouth so playtime can begin. I hear her faint whimper, and I know her pussy is throbbing just as much as my dick is. "Patience, Kitten. You'll get yours soon." She captures her lower lip between her teeth while squeezing her legs together in an effort to stave off her lust.

I round the bed and reach into the chest, knowing exactly what I'm looking for. I have all kinds of rope from jute and hemp, to cotton and nylon. And many are dyed in beautiful, vibrant colors that allow me to make unique designs and patterns.

I know any choice from my collection would not only effectively bind Quinn the way I want, but all of them would look stunning against her smooth, light brown skin. She's the perfect canvas for Shibari. And she's all fucking mine.

I gather several bundles of cotton rope in varying lengths in a deep amethyst color—a color I've chosen specifically for her. Purple is for royalty and Quinn most certainly should be treated like a queen. She reigns control of her everyday life. I want this to be her safe place, where she can relinquish that control and give it all over to me, knowing I'll do anything and everything to take care of her. She deserves that and so much more.

My mind floods with various poses I want to bind her in, but all of that will just have to wait. The best I can do tonight with my minimal patience is going to be a double-column tie to secure her to my bed and a quick body harness, because I'm dying to see this beautiful rope against her smooth skin.

I lay the ropes on the bed before offering her an outstretched hand to help her sit up. She places her delicate palm in mine as I pull her to stand in front of me. There's a moment of disbelief as I stare at the most beautiful girl in the world standing right here in my own bedroom.

"I'm going to undress you and then I'm going to bind you." My dick twitches with impatience, but I will the fucker to calm down. "I may rush through my ties tonight, but I'm going to relish every damn second I have you naked in my presence. Do you understand?"

She nods her head in agreement, but that won't do. "Consent is always verbal, Quinn."

"Yes, Mason. I understand." Her eyelids are heavy as she watches my mouth. *Oh, the wicked things I'm gonna do to you with my mouth, Kitten.*

"If there's something you don't like, tell me. Our safe word is simply *stop*. Say that word and I'll stop immediately."

"Yes, Mason." Her tone is seductive, and I know she's aroused. I can smell her delectable scent from where I stand, and I want nothing more than to drop to my knees and breathe her in—to commit her unique essence to memory.

I lean in for a kiss, capturing her lips with mine as her hands instantly wrap around my neck. I thoroughly explore her mouth before nipping at her lower lip and pulling away to undress her. As more and more of her flawless, taut skin comes into view, my thick, heavy cock leaks precum from the tip. I know I need to move this along before my dick explodes in my pants.

My fingertips lightly skate along her delicate flesh, and I'm pleased to see her skin break out in goosebumps from my touch. I ghost my mouth along her collarbone, then reach for my bundles of rope to bring them closer. I turn her body away from the bed to face the huge floor-to-ceiling, decorative, framed mirror I have leaning against my wall. I want her to see everything I'm doing to her.

With my balls aching for release, I swiftly but efficiently fashion a body harness from two long lengths of rope. I combine them into a simple but ornamental pattern of double-coin knots, tied in equidistant locations across her torso.

And though I'm working as quickly as I can, I'm mindful not to neglect the sensuality of what we're doing. I make sure with each pass of twisted cotton across her delicate skin, I lick, and kiss, and touch as much as I can. I can tell she enjoys what I'm doing because her nipples are as hard as diamonds, the scent of her arousal has intensified, and her chest heaves with each breath.

I finish the harness, knotting it at her lower back. I stand behind her, so she can see my work in the mirror.

"You look fucking gorgeous in purple, Kitten," I whisper in her ear, her head leaning back against my shoulder as she watches me.

My hands move to the front of her body, finding her large, full breasts that more than fill my palms. I massage her supple flesh, firmly brushing across her nipples with my hands. Watching us in the mirror, as I tease her perfect tits while kissing and sucking on her silky skin, has my cock hard enough to hammer nails. I know she feels it because she wiggles her round ass against it, the knots of her harness rubbing roughly between us.

I curl my hand around her hip, sliding it down to her exposed, bare pussy. I can see traces of her honey coating her inner thighs, and I want more of it to spill from her. With her eyes on mine through our reflections, I glide my middle finger through her soaking wet lips as she quietly inhales a gasp of air.

I lightly scrape my teeth along the sensitive flesh between her neck and shoulder while my fingers work her pussy. Her hips begin to roll into my hand, seeking that much-needed friction. I want this to last longer, but I can't wait another second to hear her moan my name as I make her come.

Teasing her clit mercilessly, I rub hard and fast circles over the swollen nub. I slide two fingers into her tight, wet heat and I almost come, experiencing her velvety-soft core clenching around me. Having my dick inside her is gonna feel like fucking heaven.

Curling my long fingers, I reach the rough spot at her front wall and her knees almost buckle, her body slightly sagging against mine. I hold her up, continuing to work her G-spot as my thumb presses against her throbbing clit.

My free hand grips one of her lusciously malleable tits, and I fucking love how pliant it is in my grasp. I tug and pinch her hard nipple while sweeping back and forth across that magic spot inside her. Her pussy clamps down on my fingers as she comes hard, yelling my name and her honey dripping out of her and down her thighs.

I kiss her neck, licking the tendon that runs up the side before tugging her earlobe between my teeth. She's coming down so I remove my hand, amid her dazed but incredulous protests. Her eyes widen as she watches me bring my drenched digits to my mouth and lick them clean.

"You taste better than I could've dreamed, Kitten." Our eyes are locked on each other in the mirror, and the intensity of the moment is enough to do me in.

I need her. *Right fucking now.*

I reach for more rope, so I can bind her wrists together in a double-column tie, making it easy for me to secure her to the bed. Once her wrists are bound, I kiss each of her palms before scooping her up in a bride's carry and laying her in the middle of the bed.

Scooting up her body, I raise her hands above her and tie them to a steel ring embedded in the headboard. I notice Quinn's head has tipped back to watch me, curiosity obvious in her gaze.

"Do you have... metal rings... built into your bed?" She lowers her chin to look at me, and I give her a devilish smile in return.

"It's custom made, Kitten. Perfect for our kind of

play." She matches my smile as her eyes glitter from the salacious thoughts filling her mind.

I test the binds, and satisfied that they're strong and won't budge, I move back down her body, caressing her skin in feather-light touches. Now that I have her submitting to my will, the real fun is about to begin.

ELEVEN

QUINN

My nipples are painfully hard as Mason glides his fingertips across the sensitive skin of the undersides of my arms. Having my wrists bound and secured to the headboard fills me with excitement while I anxiously await his next move. I try to keep my breathing steady, but I'm so keyed up that I can feel my arousal dripping from my throbbing pussy.

You wouldn't think I'd be the kind of girl who relishes giving over control, but I do—*oh, how I do.* I'm always in control of just about everything in my life, and for a short while, I want to let go.

I'm the go-to person, the point person, the advisor, the caretaker, the planner, the creator, the leader... I have to be so many things to so many people. I never get to just relax and let someone else take the wheel and make the decisions.

I don't want to think; I just want to feel.

And even on the rare occasions, when I believed I'd found someone I could trust enough to be that person for me, I just couldn't seem to give myself over completely. There was always something in the back of my mind that kept me from fully submitting to them.

But when I'm with Mason, I want to give him everything—every part of me. Because I know without a doubt in my mind, he'll always take care of me.

No matter what was happening in my life back then, Mason was always there for me. He never judged me or hurt me or used me. He just wanted to be there for me and never asked for anything in return. I feel so stupid for not realizing just how truly amazing he is sooner than I did. But I know now and I'm not letting him go.

I lie on my back as he straddles my waist, gazing intently into my eyes. I want so badly to reach out and touch him, to put my hands on his powerful body. But I can't, and that's part of the fun.

"So, is it just going to be me who's naked, or are you going to join me?"

"You have no idea how much I'm dying to get inside that sweet little pussy of yours. I've wanted you for so fucking long." I know he's telling me the truth because I can see his thick cock tenting his sleep pants. *Damn, I wanna taste that.*

"But I have just enough control right now, and the smallest amount of patience, so I'm going to take some time to worship your body the way it deserves." My stomach quivers at his words.

I study his gorgeous face for a few seconds before my eyes rake down to his sculpted chest. I see the firm pillows that make up his washboard abs beneath the thin material of his shirt. But then my eyes become glued to that delicious cock of his, barely restrained by the flimsy material of his pants

My mouth waters at the sight, and I can't help it when the tip of my tongue slips out and slides over the inner rim of my full lips. I desperately want my hands on him, but he has my body completely restrained. All I can do right now is lie here and wait for his next move.

And thank God he doesn't make me wait too long. He leans forward bracing his hands on each side of my head, looking down at me with those lust-filled eyes. His hips have tipped forward, and his heavy cock rests against my bare mound. We're separated by a thin layer of cotton, but it's just enough to make me crave more.

"Stop rolling your hips, Kitten." I didn't even realize I was.

"Involuntary response to having a sexy-as-fuck guy rest his cock against my pussy." I intended to fake innocence, but my voice sounds sultry from my obvious desire.

"Is that right?" Mason's eyes are half-lidded as the corner of his lips tips up in a smug smile. "Let's see what kind of response I can get from this."

He stretches out across my body, keeping my legs trapped together beneath his. He engulfs one of my nipples with his hot, wet mouth while using a free hand to massage my other breast. The sinful feeling of his tongue and teeth on my tender flesh causes my sex to flutter. I arch my back, forcing more of my breast into his eager mouth as he releases a low groan, the vibration going directly to my needy pussy.

He takes his time, alternating between worshiping

each breast equally and placing hot, open-mouthed kisses on my chest. I need more, but I already know that Mason is the type of man to give me just what he wants to give me, when he wants to give it. I relax, knowing that he's the one in control and my only job is to lie here and feel everything that he's doing to me—to let him make me feel good.

One of his hands slides up to my neck, gently resting on my throat. It isn't a harmful move, but rather one of possession. I want to be his completely and let him control my body however he chooses to do so. There's power in the freedom he gives me to completely submit to him, and I've never felt sexier or more adored in my entire life.

He slinks further down my body, finally releasing my legs and separating them with his torso. He kisses every inch of my soft belly, leaving goosebumps along my skin in his wake. When he reaches the top of my pussy, he closes his eyes reverently and deeply inhales.

"I've never smelled a more intoxicating scent than your creamy, glistening pussy." I blush, thinking about him breathing me in and looking at my most intimate parts. He opens his eyes and looks up at me over the supple planes of my figure.

"Don't get shy on me, Kitten. Every inch of your exquisite body is mine now. I get to see it, taste it, touch it... And most importantly, I get to fuck it as hard and as much as I want." My eyes practically roll back, envisioning Mason's words. I imagine him pounding into me as I'm bent at the waist, with my arms restrained by colorful rope behind my back and my legs forced apart with a spreader bar.

"Whatever you're thinking right now, don't lose that thought." And without another word, Mason voraciously devours my aching pussy.

He spreads my legs obscenely wide, using his shoulders to hold them apart. His thumbs pull back my swollen pussy lips as his masterful tongue lashes at my pulsing clit. Licking from my opening all the way to the top, he flicks my plump little nub like he's enjoying his favorite lollipop. *Damn, this man knows how to eat a woman's pussy.*

My thighs tremble as Mason moans against my soaking-wet core. Inserting two fingers deep inside me, the man is determined to get me off. I tightly grip the purple cotton rope that's currently restricting me from pulling his hair and pressing his face further into my greedy sex. It's probably for the best that I'm restrained, or I'd never let this man come up for air.

My hips are flexing off the bed as I grind myself against his magical mouth. I'm so fucking close to going over that blissful edge; my vision begins to cloud and my breathing quickens to a choppy pace.

He forces my hips still by holding them to the bed with his strong, sinewy forearm, while finger-fucking me with his other hand. Once he hits my G-spot while simultaneously sucking hard on my thrumming clit, I detonate into euphoric bliss and practically convulse with endorphins.

Mason doesn't stop, even though my body is begging him to as I'm far too sensitive for that wicked tongue of his. I try to close my legs but he doesn't let me, his hands against my inner thighs forbidding my reprieve.

"I'm not done eating your pussy, Kitten. I need to drink you down one more time and then I'll give you a break." *This man is trying to kill me.* "And then I'm gonna fuck you until neither of us can see straight."

He languidly licks my pussy as I come down from my climax. "Fuck you so hard and so long we pass out, lying boneless in my bed." He nibbles and licks my shaking thighs.

"I'll let you sleep for a while, but then I'll reach for you in the middle of the night and fuck you again and again until your pussy begs me to stop." *Oh God, I want that. I've never had that.* "And then I'll gently lick your sweet pussy over and over to ease away the soreness."

My eyes close and I lick my lips, my head filled with images of what Mason has planned for me. "Tell me you fucking want me, Quinn. Tell me you're finally mine and I don't have to let you go. Not now, not ever."

"I'm yours, Mason. Always yours."

"That's real good, Kitten. Now, beg me for my cock."

TWELVE

QUINN

My legs shake as I lie on my back, gazing deeply into Mason's eyes when he tells me to beg for his cock. At that command, a small gush of wetness dribbles from my core as I desperately want his cock to fill me up. Needing him just as badly as he needs me, I give him what he wants.

"Mason..." My voice is barely more than a moan. "Please, Mason. I want you." I can see the rise and fall of my chest while I practically pant for this man. "We've waited long enough. Please give me that big cock you've been hiding from me all day." I can't help the mischievous grin that appears on my face.

His eyes instantly darken, the pupils expanding and almost completely taking over his whiskey-colored irises. His nostrils slightly flare and I swear his temperature rises a few degrees, heat radiating off his chiseled body.

His hands cradle the sides of my face as his thumb runs across my lower lip. In the next instant, his mouth comes crashing down to mine in a hard kiss, my lips parting on a small gasp. His tongue mimics what he's about to do to me with his dick and I moan, delighting in the feel of his kiss.

He pulls away far too quickly for my liking, and I whimper in protest. "I need to get inside you now. I just don't know whether I want your mouth or your pussy first."

I close my eyes at his delicious words, my mouth watering to get a taste of his cock before he fucks me stupid. He gently massages my arms, which are still restrained, and my heart melts at his thoughtfulness. Even in his current state of lust, he's still mindful of my basic needs and doesn't want to hurt me.

Satisfied that my limbs haven't gone completely numb—just pleasantly tingly—he gives my left breast a playful smack and tugs my nipple hard, before sliding off my body. *Mmm... I love this side of Mason.*

Never breaking eye contact, he stands next to the bed, rising to his full height. He's well over six feet, making me feel delicate and feminine at barely five foot three. Passion rolls off him in waves and I squeeze my legs closed, hoping to relieve the pressure of my pulsing clit.

"No." Mason's voice is commanding, but not harsh. And I find myself pausing, wanting to do exactly what he says. "Keep those pretty thighs spread for me. I wanna see what's mine and only mine."

My heart bangs against my ribs upon hearing how much he wants me. I feel so sexy under his gaze, and I hope he always looks at me this way. No one's ever looked at me the way he does.

He reaches over his head and grasps the back of his

shirt, pulling it up and off his body. He tosses it aside as my eyes widen, now that I'm finally getting a glimpse at the sculpted planes and dips of his muscular physique. This is definitely not the Mater I knew in high school.

Time seems to slow as he hooks his thumbs inside his boxer briefs and sleep pants, pushing them over his perfectly firm, round ass. Once they reach his mid-thighs, he lets them fall to the floor and steps out of the pooled material.

My mouth drops open as I blatantly stare at the monster erection Mason is sporting. I've seen a few dicks in my time, but none of them have been as long and thick and beautiful as his. I'm dying to get my mouth on it, but if he doesn't fill me up with that soon, I'm afraid I might burst into flames.

"Eyes off my dick, Kitten." I snap my gaze up to his as he holds me in a hard stare. Feeling bratty, I look back down to the object of my desire, my core pulsing when precum drips from the tip and onto the floor.

"But I thought you wanted me to beg for it?" I feign innocence but I know he isn't buying it.

"Looks like that smart mouth of yours might need a lesson."

"Don't threaten me with funishments, Mason." A low growl leaves his chest and his hands twitch at his sides.

He and I both know I'm pushing him, which is kind of hard to do considering I'm the one tied up. But he also knows I'm going to submit, because I want to give that control over to him.

Mason climbs on the bed near my feet, straddling my body again—only this time he's gloriously naked. He drags his steel pipe of a dick up my bare skin, leaving a trail of precum as he goes. I love that he's marking me, and my nipples tighten painfully at the sensual thought.

When he gets to my mound, he lingers a few moments, rubbing the smooth, velvety skin of his broad cock head over my embarrassingly wet pussy lips. I mewl at the tantalizing sensation at the same time he hisses, "Fuck".

"As much as I wanna dive right into your hot little pussy, it's your mouth that got you in trouble."

He scoots on his knees up the rest of my body until he's straddling my chest, his weight resting on his legs and not me. I'm practically panting and drooling with that huge cock staring me right in the face. The tip glistens with moisture, and I can't wait to get my mouth on it.

His eyes bore into mine as he rubs the head of his dick across my lips. His grip is firm as he taps my mouth with it a few times before saying, "Such pretty fucking lips, Kitten. Now, open."

I don't hesitate to open wide, knowing that thick cock is going to stretch my jaw beyond what's comfortable. But I don't care, I just want to feel him slide his length across my tongue and use me however he wants.

And he does just that. As soon as he enters my mouth, his taste explodes across my tongue. The clear, sticky liquid is slightly salty and a whole lot masculine as my lips struggle to wrap around his girth.

I'm trapped by my restraints and Mason's legs as he perches in front of me, his hands braced on the headboard behind me. But I don't let that stop me from giving him whatever pleasure I can. I swirl my tongue around his broad, mushroom-shaped head and flick my tongue back and forth through his slit.

"I knew your mouth would feel good on my dick." I can tell he's trying to hold back and not choke me when I see the muscles of his strong thighs flexing and tensing.

I lick the underside of his head, my tongue dragging along the throbbing vein running up the side. I want so badly to make him come for me, to see him completely lose control the way he made me come undone. So, I hollow out my cheeks and suck him harder, leaning forward to take him in the back of my throat.

My eyes begin to water and my jaw aches but I refuse to stop. I want this. I need this. I need to please him the way he's pleased me.

My pussy lips swell with arousal to the point of being almost painful as a gush of wetness seeps out of me. Sucking Mason's dick has me so delirious with heat I can feel my impending orgasm rising to the surface. Now, I'm really determined to make us both come.

I'm so lost in pleasuring Mason as much as I am in chasing my own orgasm that I'm startled when he pulls away from my mouth, his angry purplish-red head just out of reach. "Enough." His words are grated between his teeth as he reluctantly moves further back.

"The first time you make me come, Kitten, is not gonna be with your mouth."

Breathless, I object, "But I wa—"

"No. I'm gonna come deep inside your pussy first, marking you as mine from the inside out." A shudder runs down the length of my body. "Please tell me you're on birth control and I don't have to wear a condom."

"I am. And I just had my annual exam and the results were negative."

"My tests were negative three months ago, and I always use protection. But I don't ever want anything between us, Kitten. I need to feel all of you.

"I don't wanna make you uncomfortable though. So, if you want me to wrap up, I will. I'm never gonna do anything to hurt you, Quinn."

"I need to feel you inside me now, Mason. Just you… and nothing else."

He closes his eyes and breathes in deep, his chest heaving up and down. When his eyes open again, landing on mine, there's a wild, feral heat blazing back at me. His expression leaves no room to doubt what's about to happen between us, and I couldn't look away from him right now, even if I wanted to.

Mason hastily moves down my body, his large, sinewy form wedging between my parted thighs. He frames my pussy with his hands, his thumbs pulling apart my lips and exposing my sensitive, engorged nub. He looks his fill at my core, which is obscenely on display, before firmly gripping his dick and slapping my wet center with it, the sounds echoing in the room.

Releasing his cock, he pushes his hips forward, sliding his length along my slit, bumping my clit with each upward thrust. He lifts my legs and throws them over his broad shoulders, shifting my ass off the bed to slip a plush, firm pillow underneath me.

I'm at the perfect angle for him to slam deep inside

me, and I can't wait to feel the pain of stretching wide to accommodate his thick girth. My body shudders as I wait for him to give us both what we've been dying for.

He reverently touches the knots of my body harness before tugging the strands that wrap around my hips. "Keep your eyes on me, Kitten. I need to see every expression you make as you come apart for me."

"Yes, Mas—" My words are cut off when he thrusts in deep, his pelvis flush against my ass as I throw my head back and exhale in ecstasy.

"Eyes. On. Me." He holds still, giving my pussy a second to stretch around his huge cock, but still demanding I look at him. Once my gaze is locked on his and a fresh wave of honey floods my hot pussy, he knows I'm ready for him to move.

But this is not slow, romantic lovemaking. No, this is wild, passionate sex and Mason is fucking me so hard and deep I can feel him hit my womb on every thrust. And I love every second of it.

He turns his head to kiss and nibble my calf as he firmly holds my body harness, using it to pull me toward him each time he enters me. I tightly grasp my wrist restraints, holding on for dear life as Mason fucks me relentlessly.

I'm so keyed up at hearing the indecent sounds of our bodies slapping together, I'm forced to break our visual connection as my eyes roll back into my head. I'm trying like hell to hold off my climax, but the titillating sensations of Mason's mouth on my skin, combined with the pull of the harness and sensual glide of his beautiful dick, are all too much. My body explodes in a burst of pleasure as I scream his name, my orgasm consuming me.

"Fuck yes. You're so damn gorgeous when you come for me." I barely register his words over the loud rushing of blood through my ears and my ragged panting. I don't even get a moment to calm down before he slides my limp legs off his shoulders and grips my hips, flipping me over.

The pillow is now wedged beneath my pelvis, propping my ass up slightly into the air. My arms are extended straight in front of me and I turn my head, laying my cheek against the mattress. His legs rest on the outsides of my thighs while his dick is cradled between my ass cheeks.

I pull on my ropes and arch my back, popping my ass out more—*in invitation.* I'm expecting Mason to ram into me, but he spanks my ass instead. Each smack across my voluptuous flesh causes more honey to spill from inside me.

He strokes his long, hefty cock a few times before lining the head up with my entrance. Once his dick meets my waiting, wet center, he drives into me with one smooth push of his hips.

We both cry out, but this time he doesn't give me a second to relish the feel of him inside me. This time, he fucks me punishingly right off the bat, his dick dragging across my G-spot with every thrust.

I feel him all the way in my belly, exquisite heat radiating through my core. It only intensifies when he grabs my harness with both hands like he's holding reins and rides me, roughly pummeling me with his dick.

I should probably feel ashamed or embarrassed over a man using my body this way. But I don't. Not even one bit.

I feel sexy and powerful, knowing I make him lose control like this. Knowing it's my body that drives him crazy. That it's me he wants tied up in his ropes.

But most importantly, I feel free, realizing I can give myself to him completely. That he'll give me the sweetest pleasure I've ever felt. And not only will he give me orgasmic bliss, but he'll take care of my heart and my every need.

"I can't last much longer, Kitten. I can feel your walls thrumming around my dick, and I'm about to lose it. Let go and come for me, baby."

He pulls my hips up, bringing me to my knees with my chest still flush against the bed. Leaning over me, my back to his sweat-dampened chest, he clasps my rope-covered wrists. His hands tighten around me as he impales me over and over with his perfect cock.

"Come for me, Kitten. Come right the fuck now," he whispers hotly in my ear.

He licks the side of my neck before his teeth sink into the flesh above my shoulder, and it's enough to send me off into orbit as a white haze clouds my vision. I feel my silky walls pulsate around his shaft, then clamp down firmly as I continue to climax.

I float off into bliss when Mason comes, practically roaring my name, pulling tightly on my restraints, and pressing the knots of my harness into my back. I feel each rope of cum that spurts into me, and my head becomes fuzzy with euphoria. My eyes are heavy as I drift off to the sound of Mason cooing sweet words into my ear.

I've never felt so connected to anyone in my life. I doubt I'll ever have a bond like this with anyone else. And I know, right in this very moment, that I'll never let Mason Reed go.

THIRTEEN

MASON

Fucking hell, this girl is perfect. And she's all mine. All. Fucking. Mine.

Quinn has soared into orgasmic Nirvana, so I use the time to swiftly untie her and begin rubbing the circulation back into her arms. She's been restrained for a while, but she's not new to Shibari or Kinbaku, so I'm confident she would have communicated if she needed out of her restraints sooner.

Even if she hadn't said anything during my periodic check-ins, I paid close attention to her coloring and movements. And my safety shears were close by just in case. Quinn is the most important thing to me and I'd never hurt her.

And even though it's way too fucking soon to tell her, deep down, I know I love her. I always have. Ever since she bounced into my geometry class freshman year, she's owned my heart. I just didn't know to what extent. Until now. This Christmas has brought her back to me, and nothing will take her away again.

"You're amazing, baby. So perfect for me." I kiss her smooth cheek as she lies on her back, snuggled into my side. "I'm never letting you go, Quinn. Not ever again."

I glide my fingertips fluidly across her silky skin, reveling in the feel of it beneath my touch. The combined scent of our sex and orgasms mixed lightly with sweat is heady and intoxicating. I breathe in deep, wanting to commit the fragrance to memory.

I trail my caress across her delicate collarbone, slowly dragging it down her chest and circling her nipple that's taut from the cool air. She must still be sensitive, because my graze over her firm peak causes her to stir and come back to me from her dreamy state.

"Mason Reed. What did you do to my body?" Her voice is sleepy as a slow smile spreads across her beautiful face.

"I might have fucked you unconscious. But I think you enjoyed it." I lean in and lazily kiss her sweet mouth, addicted to her unique taste. A soft moan comes from the back of her throat as she reaches up and spears her fingers into my dark, sex-disheveled hair.

"Your arms okay? I didn't have you restrained too long, did I?"

"Mmmm... not at all. I enjoyed every delicious second of it." She unconsciously begins rolling her hips into me and my cock perks up, ready for round two. "But can we take the harness off now? I want to see all the rope kisses you've given my skin."

"You wanna see my marks on you, Kitten? Is that it?" She looks up at me from her supine position, a flicker of shyness glittering in her eyes. "It pleases me immensely to know I've marked this flawless skin... but that I've also marked this pussy. My pussy. Isn't that right, Kitten?"

She hums in agreement, but I want the words. "Tell me, Quinn. I wanna hear you."

"Your pussy, Mason. Only yours." Damn right, it is.

I snake my hand down between her pretty thighs, finding her slippery, soaked folds. I slide my middle finger into her sensitive opening, the unexpected sensation causing her to gasp.

"Mason! What are you doing?" Her chin lifts as her head tilts back and her eyes close in pleasure, her hips rocking, seeking more of my touch.

"I'm pushing my cum back inside you where it belongs." I capture her mouth with mine and kiss her passionately, my desire to have her again quickly going from a low simmer to a full boil. "Let's take these ropes off, so I can see my other markings.

"You're just one step above caveman, aren't you?" Her words may be teasing, but she's still grinding her pussy against my hand.

"But you like it, Kitten. At least that's what your pussy is saying right now."

"Shut up, Mason, and fuck me again." She pulls my head toward hers and kisses me deeply.

I don't need to be told twice. I'm gonna keep her tied up and thoroughly fucked for the rest of our lives.

EPILOGUE

QUINN

1 Year Later

The last year has been a dream come true. Being with Mason is more than I could've ever imagined, and now I feel like I have everything I've ever wanted. I have an amazing job, a hot-as-fuck boyfriend, and we just moved to the top floor of our apartment building in a corner unit that overlooks downtown. It may have been almost ten years since we'd seen each other, but as soon as we met again, it was like no time had passed at all.

He's sweet and kind and sexy, wickedly smart and funny. And the sex is positively amazing. *Swoon!* We both share a love of Shibari and Kinbaku and have joined a local rope studio, where we can practice and even play if we feel like it. I finally have everything I've ever wanted and I couldn't be happier.

And this Christmas, we're definitely making it back home. We'll spend Christmas Eve and Christmas morning with my parents, then Christmas night and the day after with his. But tonight, Christmas Eve Eve, is ours —our own special holiday we've decided to celebrate with just the two of us. I know he's planned some pretty traditional festivities for tonight, but I have something else in mind.

I cut out of work early and stopped by the gourmet market on my way home. We're definitely going to work up an appetite, and we'll need plenty of snacks and refreshments on hand. If there's one thing I've learned, it's that we're both ravenous after a scene.

But tonight isn't a formal session. It's the Christmas season, so of course, we're doing something that fits the mood. I check the time on my phone and note that I have about three hours to get everything ready. It'll be tight, but I can't wait to see Mason's face when he gets home.

I prepare a huge charcuterie board with fruits, cured meats, and several artisanal cheeses that we can nibble on all night and pop it into the fridge. I bring out our favorite bourbon from our small wet bar and place the decanter and two fresh glasses on a mirrored tray on the coffee table, where I have no doubt we'll end up later tonight, watching the city lights twinkle against the dark sky.

Loading up a three-tiered dessert tower, I display plates of Christmas cookies, petit fours, and various truffles. I know it's decadent, but it's Christmas. Calories be damned!

Heading to the bedroom, I take off my work clothes and discard them in our oversized walk-in closet. Although we're not doing anything formal, I still take my time preparing my body as if we were. After exfoliating and shaving every inch of my skin, I heavily moisturize, using the peach-scented lotion I know he loves.

I unlock our chest, where we store all our ropes, and select bundles of nylon of various lengths in shades of Kelly green, Christmas red, and sunshine yellow. I've been practicing this design for a few weeks now, trying to get it just right. I had originally planned to fashion a hobble skirt and a matching chest harness, but I think he's gonna like this better.

I take my time binding myself, making sure the ropes are tied perfectly, lying smooth and untwisted against my skin. I started self-tying years ago when I discovered it calmed my stress and anxiety. The designs and knots give me something to focus on, relaxing the raging thoughts in my head. And the compression and restriction of the bindings make me feel centered, secure, and peaceful. Plus, Mason gets so turned on watching me tie myself up that I get the added bonus of mind-boggling sex when I'm done.

It takes me just over an hour to get all tied up, and I sit on the bed, my legs in pike position as I wait for Mason to get home. I timed it just right because I only sit quietly, reading on my phone, for less than five minutes when I hear him call out, "Babe, I'm home. Where are you?"

"I'm in here, honey!" I shout loud enough for him to hear me from where he stands in the living room. Immediately, I toss my phone on the nightstand and wiggle to the foot of the bed, so my ass is close to the bottom. I lie on my back and lift my bound legs straight into the air and excitedly wait for Mason to find me.

I feel like a holiday mermaid with my legs essentially bound together in a giant double-column tie from hip to ankle. But I'm positive this is going to bring a big smile to my man's face. And that's one of the best Christmas presents he can give me.

I know the moment he enters our room, because I hear a loud belly-laugh and the sound burrows deep in my heart. I'm so thankful I found the one person who not only gets me, but lets me be one hundred percent myself, even when I'm being crazy and ridiculous.

"So... is this our new Christmas tree? Because I'm pretty sure you shouldn't be on display for guests or showcased in our window." I feel his fingers graze my exposed skin, and quiver at his sensual touch.

"I'm your own private Christmas tree tonight. What do you think?"

I bound my legs in the green nylon rope and topped it off with yellow bindings around my heels and ankles, mimicking a star. The red rope was woven throughout the green, in a zig-zag pattern resembling tinsel, and knots were tied at varying intervals to imitate ornaments. Then all I had to do was lie back and point my feet to the ceiling and *ta-da*, I'm a Shibari Christmas tree.

Although, I am completely naked, so Mason's right—I should not be on display for all the world to see. Nope, this tree is for his eyes only. Especially when I'm pretty sure I know what's about to happen to his *tree*.

"I can't believe you did this just for me, Kitten." His voice has dropped an octave and taken on a sultry tone. "I thought Santa was good to me when he brought you back into my life last Christmas. But now, he's given me my own sexy-as-fuck Shibari tree." He slides his fingertips along my bared slit and my legs begin to tremble.

"Hmmm... What to do with this precious gift that I've been given." Mason tosses his gray suit jacket onto the chair by my reading nook, before walking over to the dresser to remove his cufflinks and tie. He quickly discards his black button-down shirt on the floor before walking around the side of the bed, so he can see my face.

I'll never get tired of seeing this gorgeous man and his perfectly chiseled body covered in smooth, golden skin. He steeples his hands together in front of his chest, drumming his fingertips in a rhythmic pattern. The movement causes his biceps to flex and highlights his corded, spectacularly veined forearms. *Damn, I'm a sucker for arm porn.*

I swallow hard, but lie as still as I can, waiting patiently for whatever he wants to give me—showing him I'm submitting to him completely, which is something we both crave. He sits on the edge of the bed next to me, gazing intently. I hold his stare, watching his desire flame in his beautiful eyes.

My core begins to lightly twitch as his hand reaches toward me, drawing lazy circles across my chest and around my nipples. He leans down and gives me a chaste kiss, knowing we both want more than that. But he's enjoying teasing me, wanting to bring me to that sharp edge, over and over, before letting me come.

"So many things I could do with my present." He leans down and languidly licks across the tip of my nipple before blowing gently on my dampened skin.

"Should I unwrap it first, or keep the pretty packaging?" He gives my other nipple the same treatment and my belly begins to tremble.

"Either way, you're going to be fucked. Hard. So very... very hard." My eyes close as my breathing quickens, my pulse picking up its pace. "Tell me, Kitten. Are we going to be nice?" He sweetly kisses my neck while inhaling my peachy scent. "Or are we going to be naughty this Christmas?" He bites down on my tender flesh, and I cry out at the sensation. Pulling back, he looks deeply into my eyes, waiting for my response.

I tell him exactly what he wants to hear, what I desperately want to say. "I wanna be naughty. Very naughty, sir." A sexy smirk turns up the corner of his mouth. "Merry Christmas, Mason. I love you."

"I love you more, baby. More than you'll ever know."

THE END

Want more Mason & Quinn? Check out this link to get a hot and steamy bonus scene!
https://BookHip.com/GKTSDGF

THANK YOU!

From the bottom of my heart, thank you for reading my book! I'm just a true Southern girl, reading and writing books, asking you to love me. I hope my mix of romance, with a dash of swoon, and a pinch of smut brings a smile to your face and a tingle to your fun bits.

If you enjoyed my book, please consider leaving a review on Amazon, Goodreads, BookBub, etc. Even if it's just a sentence or two about what you liked most about my book, it will help my work be seen by other readers.

FIND ELYSE KELLY

Sign up for my **NEWSLETTER** to receive updates about upcoming releases, exclusives, giveaways, and more!
https://bit.ly/2WoABd5

AMAZON: https://amzn.to/36gI26a
BOOKBUB: https://bit.ly/3kgNpaY
GOODREADS: https://bit.ly/33aUAKn
TIKTOK: https://bit.ly/37LISWU
INSTAGRAM: https://bit.ly/3izpaTh
FACEBOOK: http://bit.ly/3jaC4JA
SMUT ARMY: https://bit.ly/3D2vSMc
SMUT BRIGADE: https://bit.ly/3jplTZe
EMAIL: elyse@elysekellybooks.com

OTHER BOOKS BY ELYSE KELLY:

The Magnolia Spring Series

Welcome to Magnolia Springs! If you're looking for laugh out loud moments with lots of swoon and sexy book boyfriends, then you've come to the right place!

All the books in this series are complete standalones featuring a different couple, each with a HEA! You can enjoy these books in any order.

THE SWEET SPOT

DON'T DATE YOUR ROOMMATE

MY FAKE BOYFRIEND

There's also a sweet, spin-off standalone featuring another couple with ties to Magnolia Springs! Read their hot, friends-to-lovers romance that's sure to make you fall in love!

WANTING MY BEST FRIEND

The Heated Novella Series

Each book in The Heated Novella Series can be read as a complete standalone. These are fast, sexy, reads featuring hot alpha males that keep you nice and heated all the way through to the happy ending.

MAKING HER MINE

ALL FOR YOU

More Than Money: Billionaire Romance Series

13 authors contributed individual books to the More Than Money Series, each of which can be read as a complete standalone. This series will have you swooning over these sexy billionaires with big wallets and even bigger hearts!

So, grab a fan and a cool drink, because it's about to get hot in here!

MR. ARROGANT: A BILLIONAIRE ROMANCE

Kismet Cove Singles Week Series

Eleven authors are bringing eleven brand new stories about finding love in all sorts of way and how the charm of this lake town brings people together. Known for its delightful allure, Kismet Cove is the perfect background to find the one!

TRIPPED UP

ACKNOWLEDGMENTS

To my amazing family, thank you for supporting me and each and every passion I've wanted to pursue. You always encourage me to do whatever makes me happy, and I'm so grateful to have you all. I love you and I hope I make you proud each and every day.

To Kat, Carissa, Michelle, and the KU Steamy Romance Reads Crew, thanks for helping me make this the most amazing manuscript for my readers! You guys not only helped me make my book better, but your support is beyond anything I could have ever expected.

To Jamie, Monique, and Kala of Cover2Cover, thank you for all you do to help me run my business, so I can focus on writing. You ladies take care of everything, and I know I couldn't be in better hands than with you. I seriously couldn't do what I do without you.

To my author friends, who provide invaluable advice and an offer to be my sounding board, thanks for EVERY-THING! I would never have been brave enough to pursue my passion without you, and I would have no clue what I'm doing without your help along the way.

To Team Cactus, you girls are my Ride or Die bitches! You keep me sane in the midst of all of life's chaos and anyone who has a problem with one of us can get fucked in the ass with a cactus! If you know, you know!

To The Peen Posse, thank you for giving me a safe place to just be me. You guys have been my support, my cheer-leaders, my friends, and so much more. I'm beyond thankful for each and every one of you.

To my Smut Army and Smut Brigade, thanks for helping me get my book baby out there to so many people! You have gone above and beyond to spread the word about my book, and I'll forever be grateful for you.

To all the readers, bookstagrammers, and bloggers, thank you for reading, reviewing, and promoting my books. I wouldn't be here without you, and I'm so thankful for each and every one of you.

Turn the page for a sneak peek at

Making Her MINE

The Heated Novella Series
Available now through Amazon and
free in Kindle Unlimited!

Making Her Mine

Heated Novella Series Book 1

Copyright © 2021 by Elyse Kelly

Cover Design: FuriousFotog

Editing: Pagan Proofreading

ISBN: 9798714517457 (print)

DREW

"Mr. Cohen, you have a call from Ms. Layla Malone? She says she's been trying to reach you on your cell." My administrative assistant's voice cuts in over my speaker phone while I sit at my desk.

Pressing the button on the keypad, I respond, "She has, and I blocked her number this morning. Please tell her to stop calling. You know how to handle these calls. Follow the normal protocol." Releasing the button, I relax back in my leather chair.

"Yes, sir. I'll let her know. I'll alert security as well. Anything else?" She's asking without asking if she needs to contact security at my penthouse, but the answer is no. It's always no because I never take them home with me.

"No, Carol, that'll be all. Thank you." Yes, I'm a cold bastard. But you don't get to where I am in this world without being this way.

Layla Malone is just one of many in a long line of one-night-stands. A beautiful socialite I slept with once, a few weeks ago. I'd seen her at several fundraisers and galas, and while I knew she was interested from the very beginning, I had kept my distance. She came on too strong for me and I could tell she might be a stage-five clinger.

I made sure to spell out the rules clearly and repeatedly right from the start, but obviously she heard what she wanted to hear. Hence the numerous calls to my cell afterwards and now the calls to my office. If she continues, I'll have her socially blacklisted. I don't have time to play games like that, but being a tech billionaire requires me to protect myself and my image.

Being the CEO of my own company didn't come without a fuck-ton of blood, sweat, and tears. I wasn't born into this world, but I damn sure fucking clawed my way in, and no one is going to take it away from me. So, yeah, I may be a fucking asshole, but I have to be to keep my place in this ever-evolving industry—which will eat you up, spit you out, and forget you ever fucking existed.

I'm not just a tech genius, but I'm also a cold, cunning shark in the boardroom—I'm not arrogant; these are just facts. I'm also known for being a growly bastard because I won't be led around by my dick or my heart. I take what I want, when I want it, and I will not accept any excuses. *This* is who I fucking am—take it or leave it.

Coming from nothing, I worked my ass off to have what I have. People see the money and the lifestyle and they think it was all given to me. *The fuck it was! I made this!* Men envy me and women want to be with me. They see my good looks and they think they can snag the unattainable, wealthy bachelor. But I don't do romance or relationships—just one night.

The rules are clear from the get go. There are no pretty lies that I'm going to call them because I won't. I won't be spending the night and they damn sure won't be coming over to my place. They get one night, and one night only—no repeats and no clingers. I've never had to blacklist anyone, but the threat alone is enough to make them go away. Just the thought that they won't get another invite to the "social event of the season" is enough to have them running away in their Louboutins.

My black cell phone vibrating on my desk pulls my attention away. Reaching over, I lift it up to see my best friend's name—who is also my CFO—on the screen. Pressing the green button, I answer the call. "What do you want, dickface?"

"Wow, to be a thirty-year-old billionaire, you still act like you're seventeen. And you must be alone because you called me *dickface*," Thomas says with humor in his voice.

"Aren't you observant?" I deadpan.

"You may be my best friend, but you're still an asshole."

"Then why are you calling me?" I ask. I look at the time on my computer screen and note that it's almost four o'clock on Monday afternoon. He's normally still in the office at this time, which makes me wonder why he's calling and didn't just walk in, especially since his office is around the corner from mine. Before I can ask, Thomas cuts in.

"I need a favor, man." He can't see me, but I raise my brow in suspicion. *This ought to be good.*

"Is that right? You don't ask me for favors often, so this must be good. What do you need?"

"My sister, Elissa, is coming to the city on Thursday and needs a place to stay for the weekend." He pauses and I wait him out. I've learned in business to just keep quiet and let the other party talk. Let them lay all their cards on the table first before you make a deal. "I don't want her to stay in a hotel in a strange city all by herself."

"I think you're being ridiculous. She's not a minor. I'm pretty sure she can stay in a hotel like a big girl," I tell him.

"I know she's not a kid, but she's my baby sister and I don't like the idea of her coming to the city alone and staying in some hotel all by herself. Yes, I'm being an over-protective bastard but I'm her big brother. I'd feel safer if she stayed with you."

"And why can't she just stay with you?"

"Because you sent me to San Francisco, dumbass. I'm overseeing the acquisition this week that *you* didn't want to do yourself." *Oh, yeah, I forgot about that.*

"Okay, but why can't she just stay at your place?"

"Because I'm doing some renovations while I'm gone." I hear Thomas blow out an exasperated sigh, clearly annoyed with me. "What's the big deal, man? You live in a fucking penthouse with plenty of space. Just show her around for a few days while she's there and I'll be there on Sunday to pick her up."

What he's asking really isn't a big deal to normal people, but I'm not a normal person. I like my space and I like my solitude. With the exception of Thomas, who's been my best friend since college, I don't really allow many people to get close to me. I find people are... disappointing and I prefer to do without them, rather than having to worry about them letting me down.

"Look, man, I know you aren't big on the whole family thing because your family is a bunch of assholes —which is saying a lot considering you're the biggest asshole I know—"

"I had to learn from someone," I joke with him.

"Keep telling yourself that. But seriously, my family is awesome. We've been friends for almost a decade and you've somehow managed to avoid meeting them. They're not monsters. And my sister is cool as shit. She's kinda shy and quiet—a book nerd really—but we're really close, even though she's five years younger.

"Do this for me, man. You owe me. Don't act like I haven't had your back all these damn years. Shit, I wouldn't even be out of town right now if it weren't for you."

"You're getting paid a shit-ton of money right now, so quit complaining," I remind him.

"I'm not complaining. I'm just saying that I'd be home this week when Elissa came to visit. But since I'm not, you're the next best thing. Now quit being a dick and help your best friend out."

"Fuck, fine already. If you'll quit whining about it, I'll do it. Just text me the details."

"Aww, you're the best friend ever. I—" I hang up on him. I may have a lot of money and I may be a grown ass man, but when it's just me and my best friend, we're still just two idiots.

I inhale a deep breath and blow the air through my

mouth, closing my eyes as I try to relax. Leaning back in my black leather desk chair, I think about what I've just signed up for. The idea that I'm going to have some girl following me around like a puppy for a few days is enough to make my skin crawl.

I don't know anything about this girl. What if she's a slob? What if she has annoying habits like drumming her fingers on the table or picking her teeth? What if she talks too much? What the fuck have I gotten myself into?

Making Her Mine is now available!

Elyse Kelly

PANTY MELTING ROMANCE WITH A HAPPILY EVER AFTER.

Printed in Great Britain
by Amazon

14911301R00068